THE DUTY OF FARROWLINE

BOOK FIVE: THE PACK OF FARROWLINE SERIES

Copyright © A L Rojo 2026

The moral right of the author has been asserted in accordance with the Copyright Amendment (Moral Rights) Act 2000.

All rights reserved. Except as permitted under the Australian Copyright Act 1968 (for example, fair dealing for the purposes of study, research, criticism or review) no part of this publication may be reproduced, stored in a retrieval system, or transmitted in any form or by any means, electronic, mechanical, photocopying, recording or otherwise, without the written permission of the publisher.

 A catalogue record for this work is available from the National Library of Australia

https://www.nla.gov.au/collections

Title:	The Duty of Farrowline
Series:	The Pack of Farrowline Series
Volume:	Book V
Author:	Rojo, A L
ISBNs:	978-0-6488690-9-2
Subjects:	FICTION: Romance/Paranormal/Shifters; Fantasy/Romance; Romance/Fantasy; Fantasy/General

This story is entirely a work of fiction. No character in this story is taken from real life. Any resemblance to any person or persons living or dead is accidental and unintentional. The author, their agents and publishers cannot be held responsible for any claim otherwise and take no responsibility for any such coincidence.

Cover concept by A L Rojo
Cover design and layout by Ally Mosher at allymosher.com
Cover images used under licence from Adobe Stock and Envato Elements
Interior formatting by Katelyn at Design by Kage

THE DUTY OF FARROWLINE

BOOK FIVE: THE PACK OF FARROWLINE SERIES

A L ROJO

ALSO BY A L ROJO

The Pack of Farrowline Series

The Heart of Farrowline
The Power of Farrowline
The Strength of Farrowline
The Pride of Farrowline
The Duty of Farrowline

Shifters of Azanir Series

The Lost Lady of the Darkwoods

Author Note

The Duty of Farrowline is a MFM paranormal romance that contains themes of loss of a parent/family members, murder, a medical emergency, near drowning, adult content, explicit language, grief and violence.

Please head to www.alrojo.com.au for all content warnings and information.

To every person who knows what sacrifice and duty truly means.
You deserve love and happiness.

Pack is Pack.

Chapter One

Nicolette is Nineteen

I'd rather be anywhere than here right now!

Pouting like an adolescent, I huff and stomp my feet loudly through the forest, uncaring that I was told to be quiet. I have so much work to do for my portfolio and I don't care that Mum is upset that I was out past curfew last night. I was studying!

She doesn't seem to care that I was sitting in a library, getting my portfolio ready before I head off to university. It's my only focus right now and my one priority before I travel to Blighton to stay with my aunt and uncle, my mum's sister and her mate.

The university in Blighton is small but their art program is the best in the world. They specialise in every form, from watercolours to sketch. All the things I love. They even have an art gallery there that houses some of the most famous pieces. It also helps that I love my mum's birthpack, Rhiattline, and they've already agreed to let me stay with them for the four year course I'm hoping to enrol in. Dad has already spoken to the Alpha of Rhiattline.

I still can't believe that I'm in trouble and have to shadow Dad for the rest of the day instead of going out with the group of packmates who organised a trip to the beach. Mum took Sara.

Dad just walks beside me, keeping pace despite the fact that he has a great deal to do today and having me slow him down is probably not what he had planned for his day too. If I'm being honest, I'm acting a little like a pup, going as slow as I can, just to make him mad. It's better than the cool and calm that he is right now as he hums a perfect tune that has me regret how badly I spoke to Mum last night. It's a song has me step over and slip my hand into his large one. My dad takes it without a word and looks down, still humming and smiles warmly at me. I love my dad more than anything in this world.

We're deep in territory, in a section I'm not allowed to visit much. We can only be here if we're on training exercises with the older dominants to learn about the position we will hold in pack when we get older. It doesn't matter that I'm an adult now, Dad's main focus in Pack is to make sure we are all given time to explore as young adults and learn who we are before we have to take up important positions in Pack.

Dad said that he has to check something out near territory lines so that's why we're here.

'Lette, you know that you need to listen to curfew, yes? It doesn't matter that you're grown now and are ready to leave us to go to university.' Dad is the only one that gets to call me Lette.

'Dad, I—'

'Lette,' he cuts me off and I know that tone. It's the tone of my Alpha. I sigh, knowing I *have* to listen. 'I know you're strong and independent, and one day you'll come into your power as a dominant female. But honey, you have to listen to your mother and the rules in Farrowline. We all have to live by them. It keeps everyone safe. You have a special role here in Pack, Lette. You're a Farrow, a leader, and your role here is to maintain Pack and care for everyone while you are in territory. One day, you might decide to leave your birthpack and go on adventures but until then you have to remember your role. Your brother will one day be Alpha when he's older and wiser.'

'I can never see Tobias as Alpha or being older and wiser.' I snort. 'He's so obsessed with making Farrow Group successful.' I can't help the exasperation in my tone. Tobias spends all day in the city and all night partying with Dom, Oliver, Easton and Jax. Those males are inseparable and self-absorbed in their own lives. It annoys me that they can do whatever they want and *I* have a curfew. No one gets mad at them for not coming back to den most nights.

'Sweetheart, you'll find your way in the world. Farrowline will always be here to support you. Just like we are here for your brother and the others.'

Kicking at the littered floor, feeling a little reprimanded, I nod and agree. 'I know.'

'Oh, and Lette.' I look up and smile at the love he's radiating. His large hand comes up and cups my cheek. 'I love you.'

'I love you too, Dad.' My heart expands under his affection. My wolf does a happy dance in my body and I laugh at the feeling. I'm still getting used to feeling her so much, it seems every day I form a deeper connection with the beast under my skin. But all that dies when the energy around my dad changes dramatically and his gaze flies to something in the distance.

I look over at what's caught his attention and see a line of males watching us. They give me the creeps and I step closer to my dad's back when he rises to his full height and asks for them to declare themselves. His hand is wrapped around my arm, keeping me close and hidden from the males.

'We are here to request a Meet with Caleb Farrow, the Alpha of Farrowline. My name is—'

I miss what he says next as I'm too focused on the way dad's hand morphs into claws.

Ears straining, I try to stay focused on the words the weird male is saying. 'We request a Meet and will follow the rules.'

I watch as one of them cuts his hand and gives a blood oath.

'We are from the Pack of Vestraline.'

Dad nods and I look up at him with worry. Something doesn't feel right. 'I will honour the rules of the Meet. Welcome to Farrowline,' Dad states, still in alpha-mode. He bends down then and his honey coloured eyes capture mine. I can see his wolf staring back at me and I know I have to listen. 'Nicolette, I want you to run back to den, okay. Fast.'

I don't understand what's happening but I nod, unable to not agree. 'Yes, Dad.' I hesitate. 'I can help though. Stay here with you. I can handle myself.'

His eyes soften and he nods along with me. 'I know you can, but I need you to go back to den.'

I can't argue with my alpha. 'Okay.'

'Good, now. Don't come back, no matter what you hear. Do you understand Lette? Do not come back here. I'll come find you.'

I can't help but hesitate and look over at the strange line of males. Something is wrong, I can tell.

'Go, honey.'

I take off into the forest and don't stop even when I hear my dad howl a call to the leaders of Farrowline.

Too confused, I slam into a body and feel arms wrap around me. I'm picked off my feet and held close while I draw in the comforting scent of my Beta. I don't know if I'm overreacting but I don't like the feeling in my gut. The one that has my mostly calm wolf battering against my skin.

'Nicolette, what's happened?'

My words are hurried and breathy as I tell my Beta and another member of the Circle what is going on. The Beta plants me back on my feet and tells me to run and get everyone in their dens.

That's when I hear it.

Two distinct cracks.

A sound that will forever haunt me. A sound that had my Beta run, yelling at me to get back to den and not stop.

A sound that changes my life forever.

Chapter Two

Present Day

Fingers flying over the device on my lap, I type up an important contract while I consider the list of things that I have to do before noon.

The sun is barely up and the colours of morning spill into the oversized windows of the office. The cityscape at this time of day is stunning and I refuse to acknowledge the ridiculousness of my situation right now, so I work.

Cracking my neck, I take a breath and start massaging the ache in my shoulder. The last few days have been an absolute whirlwind.

A sharp knock at the door has me drop my hand from my sore body and start typing again.

'Come in,' I call and check the time on my device with a smirk. 'It's a bit early, August.' He wasn't supposed to be here until eight, at least I don't think he was. I'd have to ask him what time he starts. He manages the schedule—mine, his, every employee under me.

'Yes, it is,' the tall, lean, well-dressed male replies and I can hear the judgement in his tone.

His dark, pinstriped suit is new and I can't help but remember the way he dressed five years ago when he showed up at my office looking for someone to give him a chance. A male with no skill, in a new city, and looking for more than just a job. I remember that day so distinctly. He was looking for Pack. For community.

My personal assistant doesn't hide the way he runs those pale eyes over my position on the couch or the small bag of clothing beside it. 'So, you're still hiding out in your office.'

I continue with what I'm doing. 'I'm not hiding.'

His, 'mmmhhhmmm,' says a great deal as he sits gracefully in the single black leather seat across the meeting space in my office.

This place is practically a small apartment anyway and in one of the best buildings in South Sylo, so it's not so bad staying here.

'It's been three days.'

'*And?* I don't have to explain myself to you,' I state, looking over the laptop screen so that he can see the warning in my eyes.

I don't need him on my case like everyone else is. If I want to sleep in my office in Farrow Group, then I'll sleep in my office in Farrow Group.

I *am not* hiding from anyone.

August tries to hide his smirk and I consider for the second time this week if I really need a personal assistant anymore.

I have multiple assistants in every business I own and run and August manages them all. While he frustrates the hell out of me and tries to meddle with my personal life, I rely on him enough that the thought of finding someone new, and training them, has me give up thoughts of dismissing him—for now.

'You're thinking about firing me again,' August smirks. His tablet is resting on his now crossed legs and most of his attention is on whatever he's organising. Probably more events and meetings for me to attend just to annoy me.

'Yes.'

The damn male chuckles. 'How many times does that make it this week?'

'Four,' I reply casually being fully serious and he knows it. That's why he grins wide, all proud of himself. 'Is there a reason you're here this early?'

All playfulness gone, he sits up and begins to explain my day. Which consists of multiple meetings and an interview for an assistant for Jax and the accounting team. After Gilly resigned her position at Farrow Group, it's been something I need to get sorted.

Just another issue for me to fix.

I'm excited for our Pack Tracker, but honestly, the work it puts on my plate now is enough to give me a headache.

August moves around the space and disappears into one of the doors on the left.

He comes out wheeling a long rack full of clothes. He doesn't stop instructing me on my day and pulls out a sky blue business suit that I shake my head at. Even with my focus on my device, I'm so used to multi-tasking that I don't need to look up.

August puts it back and pulls out the red pant suit with the wide leg that I told him not to purchase me. I go to say no but he cuts me off by beginning to explain that my nine am meeting is with some businessman who has been hounding me for a meeting for months. He says it like it's some kind of explanation why I should pick the red outfit.

I'm actually really interested in what Carvin Henworth has to show me today. His ideas have made the pack a great deal of money. However, with everything happening right now, I'm not in the right headspace.

'Cancel it,' I reply absently, trying to read over the last few paragraphs of this contract.

'You can't,' August states, pulling the suit off the hanger and walking over to lay it on the large coffee table. 'You've cancelled this meeting five times. If you don't go, then I'll have to speak to him again and deal with his insipid assistant.'

August moves efficiently around the space, leaving a folded towel and my toiletries bag beside the suit. 'You, go shower and get ready, and I'll get Brooke to grab you breakfast on her way into the office.'

He refers to the assistant I hired after Ridley was promoted here at Farrow Group. She's here to help all the heads of departments in the company. I haven't had much to do with her really. August liked her, so that was the main reason why we hired her.

'Mama also called to say that you're expected at her den tonight for a Pack dinner.'

I don't answer and August doesn't push it. Instead, I finish off what I'm doing.

Happy with how the contract is looking, I save my work and get off the couch. I battle a groan at my stiff and sore muscles and stretch out.

'How long are you going to stay here? Is this really how you should handle the situation?'

'Yes,' I sigh, grabbing the clothes August has laid out for me. Including my underwear.

I'm firing him today for sure.

'That's not how I'd handle it. If I had two males waiting for me at my den, I'd be curled up between them having all sorts of fun. Especially if they looked like your mates.'

'They aren't my anything.' I kick the door of my office bathroom closed with my foot, cutting off the deep laughter filling the space.

'Are you sure they know that, because I'm not even Farrowline and I know about your mates,' his calls from the other side of the door.

'You're fired,' I shout back and then groan when he just laughs louder.

I don't have time for this.

Chapter Three

Present Day

Finishing up on a video meeting, I say a quick goodbye to the young man on the screen who runs the advertising company I invested in a few years ago.

August is across the table in an instant, pulling containers from a bag and laying out food around all my papers and devices.

My stomach rumbles and I start picking as I pull up the next document that requires my attention.

'You have half an hour until you need to head across town. Bentley is waiting out the front to take us.'

Mouth full, I glance up, brows rising, waiting for more information about why I need to be across town and why my driver is waiting for me.

'Jennifer Sarker from the Sylo Times. She's the one who wants to do the article spread for females in business story. She really wanted you to be part of the article,' he reminds me and I remember the name…kinda.

'Did I agree to that?' I can't remember and just nod when August informs me that it's something I have to do, something about good press and coverage.

'Also, Mama called, again.'

'Just tell her I'm busy.'

The noise that fills the office has me stiffen. I wish I could swallow my words back into my mouth when a monstrous body appears in the doorway of my office.

August straightens and looks to me quickly. There isn't fear in his gaze, but trepidation. I don't blame him.

'August, could you leave us for a moment, please.' My brother doesn't wait for his reply and August nods his head in submission and leaves the office without a word.

Tobias makes himself at home. He walks in slowly, takes a seat across from me and rests his right ankle on his left knee.

Still picking at my food, I go back to my work and ignore him. 'I don't have time for this Tobias.'

He replies with a small growl. 'Nicolette, we need to talk.'

I know what he wants to talk about, and frankly, I don't see why everyone thinks this is their business. 'I'm busy.'

'You're always busy.' Every word is layered with criticism. A typical response, and one that washes over me. I've heard it all before.

'Yes, I am. So, is there a point to this conversation?' I battle with the spark of rage that lights in my chest. I have a mountain of work to do and won't get any sleep tonight if I'm not left alone.

'Nic, stop working.'

That tone. I despise that tone. It's one that makes me want to bare my teeth and tell him…to…to just leave me alone.

Instead, I stop and look over at the male sitting across from me. 'What do you want, Tobias?' I have no control over the way I snap at him.

I don't have time for this.

He doesn't reply straight away, instead he keeps his focus on my face like he's trying to work out what to say. I can see the internal struggle as he decides if he's going to use his big brother voice or his alpha one. Both very different. He decides on big brother first. 'You need to go to Farrowline and deal with the situation. It's causing quite the disruption amongst the Pack.' There seems to be more he wants to add, but he stops. I hate that it grabs my attention and has me bite my tongue to stop myself from asking what he means.

I taste blood.

Eyes narrowed in his direction, I grumble, 'I don't need to deal with anything. You're the Alpha. It's your pack. You deal with it.'

Folding those massive arms around his chest, Tobias smirks and I want to jump the table and beat him with my fists. 'They're not my mates.'

I go to tell him that I don't have mates but my throat closes up and I struggle to find the words.

It's been three days since we found two males at our territory lines. Two males who I never expected to come here after everything that happened, I don't want to see them.

I haven't voiced any commitment. Nor have I spoken the words aloud to accept any mating bond…bonds…Jeez!

It's not my fault that those males believe that what happened between us in Rhiattline was me accepting them.

That's not how it works, so they can scream that I'm their mate from the rooftop of this massive skyscraper and I still don't care.

Mates.

Plural.

What a nightmare!

'Nicolette.'

There's a warning in his tone that has me mumble under my breath that he can shove his alpha tone up his arse. Tobias just shakes his head and sighs. 'You *will* go to Farrowline tonight and you'll begin to manage this situation. I don't have the time or the energy for this. Loners have been harassing our lines and Ridley and I are trying to plan the mating ceremony that seems destined to never happen.'

The mating ceremony.

I still can't believe it's only a few months away.

Ridley tried to have a conversation with us all about cancelling the event with everything that's been happening. I agreed with the others that Farrowline has been through some massive changes and we need this celebration.

'*And* I don't need the Alpha of Rhiattline down my throat about our pack treating two of their top dominants with anything but respect.'

'They're not Rhiattline dominants,' I absently correct. They're from a country far from here. They're only visiting Rhiattline.

'Nicolette!'

'Then tell them to go back!' I half shout, rising to my feet, unable to contain myself anymore. I don't need this. I'm busy!

Tobias stands slowly as I huff and puff and clench my hands. 'I'm not asking you,' he states, leaving no room for any more argument. 'Go to Pack and deal with this, Nicolette! Running away from your problems is not going to help you this time.'

Wolf coming to the forefront of my mind, I snarl and I know she's in my eyes as the Alpha stares me down. He isn't my brother anymore and I am no longer his sister, until his face softens and his shoulder slump at whatever he sees on my face.

I'm not ready for the emotion in his tone when he says, 'I didn't mean it like that, Nic.'

He leans over the table and takes my balled up fist and holds it between his massive hands. His eyes never leave mine. 'I love you beyond words, Nicolette, but you can't pretend like this isn't happening and bury yourself in work. I sometimes fear that I failed you. That I should've handled everything better.'

I'm still too emotional to respond.

He didn't do anything wrong. We're products of our situation. Both forced to grow up quicker than we wanted and take on unimaginable responsibility.

'You deserve happiness and I truly hope that you find it.'

He brings my fist to his lips and kisses it softly as I draw in his scent to find some balance.

My emotions are rolling and I fight the need to wolf out and run.

I watch as my brother leaves and I allow myself a moment to fall apart. Just a moment, before I suck in a breath and call August in so that we can head to Central Sylo for another meeting.

Chapter Four

Nicolette is Nineteen

The sound of wailing breaks parts of my soul that I was never aware of.

On my knees, unable to move, I hold onto my sister so tightly that I'm sure I'm hurting her.

Sara cries thick tears against my thigh, uncaring of my grip. Uncaring of anything as she bleeds her heartache through the water saturating my pants. Her pain is like daggers that burrow deep into my heart. It doesn't matter that we're only a year apart in age, she is my little sister. My sweet, less-dominant sister, who I've been protecting since her birth. I wish I could shield her from this nightmare. But no matter how tightly I hold her, I know I can't fix this.

I long to cover my ears from the sound of my mother's wailing. Every noise she makes sends me further and further into the pit of despair that has formed in my chest.

He's dead.

My father.

My Alpha.

I ran away and I left him. I ran away and he was killed. So many of our packmates were killed and I don't know what that means. It's like someone has come and ignited a bomb in my happy life and I know deep down that it'll never, ever, be the same again.

My dad...*he's dead.*

There are packmates everywhere.

Mates cry and scream for their deceased. Pups mourn loudly for their fathers and I sit, rocking Sara back and forth wishing that I could wake up from this nightmare. Wishing I did more to help.

'I'm so sorry, Sara,' I whisper down at my beautiful sister. She just cries harder in my arms. 'I should have stayed with him. I should've done more.' My words are lost over the noises in the den.

I look up and say, 'I should have done more,' to the male now crouched down in front of us. Liam's familiar sky blue eyes are filled with emotion. I can almost taste the rage in the air. His grief.

'This is not your fault, Nicolette,' he says and rests his hand gently on Sara's face. My sister weeps harder and leans into his touch. His focus is on her, and only her, as she moves into his now waiting arms. Liam sits down and pulls her into his lap.

I watch my sister bury her face into Liam's neck and weep. She clings to him like he's her everything. Like he's the one that'll be able to stick her back together.

It breaks my heart even more.

The big, dominant male strokes her hair sweetly and whispers words of love and care. The connection between my sister and one of my brother's closest friends has been growing for years now. Dad said that one day Liam and Sara will realise that they're mates when we had one of our nightly walks...Dad *used* to say.

A burning sensation creeps into my throat, I look around at the chaos.

The pack healers are running around supporting where they can. Dominants try to keep their own emotions in check while comforting mates and pups. Tobias is holding our wailing mother in his massive arms, his face stoic. However, when they lift to mine, I see the rage and heartbreak.

His look screams his intentions, they scream revenge, and I close my eyes and take a breath and hope that when I open them and find him still staring that he knows I will be coming with him. He is our new Alpha as of this morning and everything has changed.

My entire world will never be the same again.

Chapter Five

Present Day

Heels clicking on the stone floor, I catch a glimpse of myself in the mirrors lining the prestigious restaurant foyer. I do look good in my red outfit, and as of right now, I'm not firing August.

'See, I told you that colour looks hot on you,' August whispers as we walk briskly, side-by-side, into the restaurant.

I give a nonchalant gesture to what he said and decide I'll fire him tomorrow.

I'm ushered to a table in the centre of the half-empty establishment and I blank on the name of the journalist again.

'Jessica Sarker,' August whispers again, reminding me, having clearly picked up that I'd forgotten. She's human and I don't worry that she can hear him or the way I state to my assistant that this better not be a waste of time. The shifter just snickers under his breath.

Jessica rises instantly when we get close and has the biggest grin on her face like she is excited to see me. I take the hand she holds out. 'Ms Farrow, thank you so much for taking the time out of your schedule to be here today. I really appreciate you.'

August pulls out my chair. 'Thank you for asking me to be part of your article,' I say, nodding my thanks to August who finds himself a seat at a nearby table.

His phone and tablet are in his hand and he gets right into work, I know he's listening though. He knows that I don't like interviews and I have limits on the kind of questions I like to discuss. Not that many reporters dare ask me any non-approved questions. Not anymore. Maybe in my early years, but they learnt quick smart that I'm not one to play games.

Jessica is all smiles. She's younger than I expected. Her blonde hair is pulled back in a messy, high pony and she fusses around with all the papers and the recording device on the table.

The waiter comes and asks us what we'd like and we both order while Jessica picks up her pen and then realises that she needs something else.

'Sorry, this is my first big article.'

She really doesn't need to tell me what I've already gathered. 'It's fine, take your time.'

The waiter appears and I fuss with my coffee, giving her some space to get over her nerves. I get this a lot. I've been told that I'm intimidating. I don't really understand, especially seeing as how I don't really spend a great deal of time socialising. I have no time for that.

Jessica finishes up and throws me an apologetic look before she tells me that she's ready. 'Okay, so, Ms Farrow, what would you say the secret to success is?'

I don't know why I expected her question to be a little more creative. That's all people ever want to know. *How to make money.*

'Hard work and dedication. I work hard,' I say on autopilot.

'You invest in a great number of start-up companies. Some that others wouldn't even touch because of the age of the entrepreneurs. You seem to not have an issue working with young people and shifters, why is that?'

Taking a sip of coffee, I nod. Again, expecting this question. 'I don't feel that age should be a factor in success. Age, means nothing.'

She nods, loving this. 'Yes, you were only nineteen when you started working with your brother, the Alpha of Farrowline. If my research is accurate, you ran Farrow Group for an entire year as the acting CEO when it was still in its early years, helping to make it the success it is today.'

She looks up from her notes eagerly. She hasn't asked me a question so I stay quiet. I can feel August tense from the table close by. He's no longer focused on his device.

Jessica's eyes sparkle and I realise that she isn't the innocent, new reporter she was portraying.

'In my research, I discovered that you began working at Farrow Group the same year your father, the previous Alpha of Farrowline, was murdered.'

I refuse to react, she isn't saying anything that I don't already know. It's my life, I had a front row seat to the story.

She's trying to get me to open up and she wouldn't be the first to try to see if I *do* have a human side.

Her biggest mistake is that I think I lost my humanity a long time ago.

Chapter Six

Present Day

'You were enrolled in art school and were set to attend. My research findings indicate that you were a great artist.'

I watch as she pulls out photos from the folder beside the recording device. All photos of an early portfolio I haven't seen in years and clearly taken from the university server I summitted it to when I was eighteen years old.

I no longer care about the reporter and the shit she is spilling. My focus is on the images that remind me of a time long gone.

Of a different life.

Of how my dad helped me put that portfolio of work together.

I remember ordering pizza and sitting on the living room floor with all my work scattered on every surface of the room while he and I walked around picking out our favourites.

It's a life that could have been. A life buried.

'I heard that you were there the day your father, Alpha Caleb Farrow, was murdered by the pack of Vestraline. Is that true? Is that the reason why you stayed in Sylo?'

August rises quickly and the human's eyes widen a little at what I'm sure is my now very angry assistant. The chuffing noise he makes at the back of his throat is enough to have her pale as August appears at the side of the table. His normally pale eyes are dark and full of rage. I should probably tell him to rein it in but you can't tell a bear shifter anything when they're in a mood.

'You were given strict instructions on the topics you could discuss. This is underhanded and tabloid journalism. How dare you disrespect Ms Farrow.'

Jessica opens and closes her mouth while August picks up the photos and places them back in her folder. Her reaction seems genuine even though I know my assistant has just given her a great story now. I can already see the headline of her 'article on females in business'.

I rise on my thin heels.

Tomorrow, the Sylo Times will read how I overreacted to simple questions about my personal life and how I became upset enough to walk out of an interview when my father was mentioned.

Poor Nicolette Farrow, the 'ice-queen business female' is too emotional for the work she does. I've done this a hundred times. Heard and read it all before.

Jessica's attention flies to me the moment I'm on my feet. 'Ms Farrow, I'm so sorry—'

'Yes, I'm sure you are,' I interrupt and indicate for August to give her back the folder. 'I don't have secrets. Any journalist can go through and find information about me, most of it is public knowledge. And Ms Sarker, I've been asked these questions. Many times. When I was younger, it was to find cracks. To show that I was a young female who was in over her head, playing business with other big, powerful males, whose egos were hurt that I was making money. Lots of money. More money than they were,' I add, just to see her snap her mouth shut.

'Then, when they eventually realised that I wasn't so easily intimidated, their stories were written to find weakness, to throw stones and hope that one would hit, and they can make their careers off getting Nicolette Farrow to cry or spill her guts, or break. I'll tell you what I've been telling others since I was nineteen. You can try to find a human interest story in my life, Ms Sarker. In fact, I encourage you to try and be creative and see if you can present a new angle to help your career advance. However, there's nothing there except gossip and what you believe to be truth. You will get it wrong. They always do. I work hard for what I have and I support my Pack and my employees off the back of endless hours and a commitment. When you want to discuss the real story about females in business, who have to work extra hard in this industry to be seen, heard and taken seriously, and how breaking that glass ceiling can cut deep but in the best possible way, then you may call me again.'

I pick up my belongings from the table, knowing I have places to be. The message from Sara, a new mother of two, who seems very upset is my priority.

I give the reporter one last look and get the desired reaction when she sits straighter as if knowing she has just been given an important lesson today. Pulling a few bills out of the wallet section attached to my phone,

I throw the notes down on the table, knowing full well that her company would be picking up the bill.

I leave enough for a decent tip to the waiter pretending to not watch our exchange and turn on my heels and walk calmly outside.

'That fucking bitch.'

'August, it's fine.'

I'm getting a headache and rub my temple.

Sighing, I stop at the back of the slick black car parked out the front of the restaurant and nod when Bentley hurries around the vehicle.

The elderly male, with his pressed suit, nods in greeting and opens the back door with a polite word.

I like Bentley. He's been my driver for a few years now. I find it hard to do business and drive at the same time so August found me Bentley, and not that I'd tell him, but I'm very grateful.

It took a lot of personal growth to concede control over driving myself around during work hours.

I hop into the car and the door is closed with a soft thud before August appears on the passenger side and gets in beside me. His fingers are moving furiously over the screen of his phone and I can only imagine the angry email he is now sending to the owner of the Sylo Times.

'I'll fucking bury her!' he growls, completely in his own world. He's going to give himself a heart attack one of these days.

'August, this doesn't matter. We've dealt with this before. She'll write some bullshit article and I'll be the topic of conversation again for a month and the world will move on to the next story,' I say to my phone.

I read the message from Sara who is asking me to come back to Pack tonight and a message from my mum saying the same thing. Tobias also left me a message informing me that I better respond to Sara and Mama.

I seriously don't have time for this nonsense and open my calendar. My temper rises at the sight of it and the two very new events that have been scheduled.

'We have more pressing things to handle like the two fundraising events that have appeared on my calendar just now!' I state through gritted teeth. These weren't there this morning and August knows how much I hate last minute events.

August throws me a professional nod as he slowly lowers his phone. 'You have two events. They were on your calendar for a month.'

'No, they weren't,' I insist. He doesn't react to my small outburst. 'I'm firing you,' I say, getting a handle on my emotions easily.

'Perfect, should I schedule that in for tomorrow or will we finally have a Saturday off?'

Smart arse.

'Keep it up and it'll be today.'

His chuckle has me snap my focus to the busy city outside my window and I smile.

It falls when I realise that I have to go to Farrowline and deal with...*them*.

Chapter Seven

Present Day

Leaning against the side of Mama's den, I watch almost in shock, at the sight before me. Standing and sitting around the backyard is a group of pack females ranging in ages from adolescent to elderly, all watching two males as they dig a deep trench.

Shirtless.

Dark tanned skin on full display.

Sweat glistening off their defined pecs and washboard abs as they work.

Both tall, lean and cut muscle.

Both unbelievably attractive in their own right.

It's like the opening of some kind of erotica film made for a female's enjoyment. And despite the entire situation I'm in right now, and why I haven't been home for days, I'd pay good money to watch that film. A film starring the two males from Rhiattline. Two dominant, very attractive and very...very, arrogant males who I met on a trip to my mother's birthpack when I was sent on a 'holiday' by Mama. A holiday we all knew was a way for her to encourage me to get away from work and maybe meet a male. There is a part of me that believes she knew what was actually going to happen. That she was fully aware that Rhiattline had two dominants visiting from a country over the seas. They've been staying in Rhiattline for a few months while the taller one's sister was becoming comfortable within the pack after meeting her mate on a vacation. The two males would never leave her unless they knew she was safe. It is a big reason why I was able to leave and come back to Farrowline and why it took them over a month to hunt me down. She got hurt and they stayed for her recovery.

I thought they'd let me go. How wrong I was.

Easton steps up beside me. 'I understand why you rang me all those weeks ago speaking about the painting you saw in the art gallery at Blighton.'

I groan at the memory of why I called him but am stopped from replying because Gilly appears at my other side whistling her appreciation for the show before us. Her blue eyes sparkle in amusement.

'Damn, girl! What're you doing over here when your males are half naked and glowing under the sunlight over there?' She points toward the peep-show that everyone seems to be enjoying.

I hate that I feel the bite of possessiveness and jealously.

I want to shout and yell and demand that everyone leaves now and stop looking.

I hope the expression I throw her over my shoulder is enough to shut her up and maybe a few months ago it would have. Not now though, something has changed in our Tracker.

Long gone is the Gilly Sommers who had little confidence and a broken heart, who regularly drank herself into a stupor and continually doubted her abilities. Now, Gilly is Gilly Sommers-Tyler, the Tracker of Farrowline, and mated female to one of our most powerful males, Oliver Tyler. A male who has helped lead our pack from the moment my father was murdered. The pair are a power couple. Gilly is the strongest Tracker in generations. Her abilities surpass everything we ever thought possible of a Tracker. Without her, our Pack wouldn't be as strong and I value her for everything she brings to Farrowline and everything she is as a female.

'Please Gilly, not now.' My tone is a little harsh but it'd take more than that to get Gilly to leave you alone.

She's not easily offended and after coming back from her 'quest' to find herself, she has been extra confident and easy-going. Could also have to do with the male that steps up behind her and casually puts his arm around her middle, hugging her close. It's been a month or so since their mating bond kicked in and you rarely see them apart or around the pack really, they spend a great deal of time up at the 'sex' cabin, or so everyone calls the once run-down dwelling the dominants used to use if they were out on patrols that far from the inner territory.

'Well, now I know where half the pack is.' Oliver chuckles and I sigh dramatically.

It's probably super weird that we're just standing on the outskirts of the group watching two dominant males digging dirt, but I don't want to leave or go over and acknowledge them, especially when I see Mama. She walks down the steps of her patio carrying a tray of drinks. She heads through the mass of chatty females to the males she's got doing her dirty work. I have no idea why she has them building a trench and watch as she places the tray down on a little table someone put beside the hole and starts to chat away to the newcomers. She's completely at ease around them despite having no idea who they are.

They've only been here for three days!

My mother probably only sees two males ready to take her troubled, overworked pup off her hands. She wouldn't care that it's nearly unheard of to have two mates.

It doesn't help that my first encounter with the two males now putting on the greatest 'two male strip show' for Farrowline was the most humiliating and embarrassing moment of my life.

Gilly and Oliver have no idea the circumstances around how I met the dominant pair.

They aren't brothers by blood.

They're connected through a bond forged in loss, danger and responsibility. Their pack had been in a territory war for nearly three decades and both males lost their families at a young age, one sister survived and is who they were following when I met them in Rhiattline. The region they were born in is notorious for battles and changing of alphas and loyalties.

The Alpha of Rhiattline was trying to encourage them to stay in the pack permanently. I thought he had succeeded. The fact that they're here now means he wasn't successful.

There was a reason why I came back here and left them behind. It was a shock seeing them a few days ago on our territory lines. I thought they wanted nothing to do with me. Our argument when I left was bad...really bad.

They're different to the wolf shifters I've come across. Yes, they're typical dominant males, with their arrogance and an almost built-in understanding that they're gorgeous, but the way they do things shocked me at first. They challenged me from the very moment I met them to consider my values and priorities.

To rethink everything I've built here in Farrowline.

Don't get me wrong, I love my pack. I work all day, every day, to support them all.

I contribute financially and ensure that everyone has what they need to survive and thrive. I'm a Farrow, and as my father told me many years ago, I have a responsibility and I've never forgotten that.

But, when I met these two males, I felt my world crumble, just like it did all those years ago when I ran away on my father's command.

Raising my hand to run my finger over the thin scar along my hairline, I'm powerless to the onslaught of memory.

On that bright, sunny morning in Rhiattline, when I made a bad judgement call and came very close to death, I met Diego Santana and Luis Cortez. They're the reason I'm standing here right now. I would've died that day if it wasn't for them.

Diego and Luis saved my life, and then promptly turned it upside down.

Chapter Eight

Nicolette in Rhiattline

Damn Mama and her meddling in my affairs!

If it wasn't for her, I'd actually want to be here in Rhiattline.

Sitting heavily on the sand, I rest my chin on my raised knees and look out at the picturesque shoreline with a longing so deep in my soul that I allow the tears to drip down my cheeks. Something I do rarely, and only ever in privacy.

I don't have the luxury to let myself fall apart. I have responsibilities and work to do and money to make. And…and, I'm exhausted.

My phone buzzes in my pack pocket.

I ignore it.

August told me that he wouldn't call until this afternoon so if it's not him, it's someone from Farrowline, and I don't have the energy to pretend with them at the moment.

Watching birds dive and dance above the crashing waves, I try to absorb the tranquillity of the beach. It's too early for anyone to be around. The landscape here is spectacular and one of the main reasons why I loved coming here as an adolescent. It has changed though over the years.

Along the forest line there is now a row of bungalow dwellings that the pack rents to tourists. They sit right where the trees meet the sand and the business female in me is very impressed. I have to meet the shifters who came up with the concept because, while it's great, their business has potential to expand and make the pack very successful.

I'll ask my aunt to point me towards the shifter who came up with the idea.

I take off my shoes and bury my toes in the grainy sand.

I only got here about an hour ago and was instructed to either pick to stay with my aunt or out here in Bungalow Three. The pink one. The others are all equally bright in colour. Their wood siding and white, arched roofs are very appealing and while they are surrounded by the nature of this place, they don't look out of place even with the 'fun' colours. There are five in total.

Aunt El told me that there are only two shifters out here at the moment with the other ones vacant while we're in the 'off season'. Tourists stay away this time of year and I look out at the violent waves crashing against the shore. The ocean here can be so peaceful, and yet, in the off season, so deadly.

I used to come here a lot when I was younger so I've been taught all about the landscape. The forest in Rhiattline is thick jungle. The native animals can be dangerous and the cliffs that hug either side of the beach are monstrous. However, despite the volatile nature, Rhiattline has always felt like home. I even planned on living here. I was going to go to art school not too far from this territory.

Thinking of it now has me so angry. Oh, to be so naive to think that life could be as easy as to go to art school and study a passion.

Hobbies aren't careers.

I wish I could go back to a time when life hadn't hardened my heart with pain and responsibility. I haven't picked up a brush or pencil in years. I probably would be shit at it if I did.

Being here in Rhiattline is difficult. There's a part of me that wants to lay in the sand like I used to when I was younger. I loved sitting just on the very edge of the shoreline and letting the water hit me as it comes into shore.

Now I sit just out of reach of the water, watching as it comes close and then creeps back into the sea.

The early morning breeze plays in my unbound hair and with a heavy trench coat on, I hug myself against the chill of it.

I didn't want to come here.

My mother forced me to travel with a group of packmates that were invited for a mating ceremony. We have lots of ties to different packs around the country. The group I'm with went to university with the female that's having her ceremony. I was asked to come along to make sure everyone was 'all right,' and let's be real, to get me out of the den and have me meet new shifters.

Maybe even find a mate...*blah!*

My mother isn't as stealthy as she think she is. Her and Maree, Dom's aunt, talk louder than anyone else. When they think no one's around, they gossip and scheme like pros. I know why they 'suggested' I come along with the group and it has nothing to do with ensuring their safety. It was to get me out of the pack and the office.

Feeling the hairs on the back of my neck stand up, I look over my shoulder at the bungalows and try to work out why my skin feels funny and why the beast under it begins to wake up.

My vision flicks between the dichromatic vision of my wolf as she allows me better range in sight and then back to human when she doesn't pick up any threats.

There's a slight movement in the front window of the blue bungalow next to my pink one. Not feeling a threat, I put it down to one of the shifters that live out here being awake and go back to studying the view.

Now, feeling antsy and unable to stay seated, I stand on bare feet, fully clothed and trudge into the water. Sucking in a curse when the icy liquid crashes into my thighs, I welcome the feeling. It's oddly refreshing, so I move further in.

Deep in my own thoughts, this place takes me back to everything I've lost and given up. All the decisions I've made since.

I continue to fight the waves, forgetting one of the biggest dangers of this beach. That the sand drops away and the sea becomes incredibly deep.

I step one last time, just as a monster wave breaks before me and I'm smashed off my feet.

Chapter Nine

Nicolette in Rhiattline

Fighting the pull of the water is incredibly hard when you're fully clothed.

I roll and roll and am jerked left and right as wave after wave slams down above me. Like a rag doll in a washing machine, I have no power over the force of the ocean and am completely at its mercy.

The way the water slams against my body hurts and when I break the surface for a second, I'm able to suck in a quick breath.

Another wave crashes in over my head, knocking it all out of my lungs.

Trying to keep my wits about me, I don't fight the rip as you're taught as a pup.

It doesn't help.

I end up hitting the sandy floor when the waves summersault me sideways. My head smacks into something sharp and I scream the reminder of the sweet air in my lungs out at the force of the impact and snap my mouth shut to stop from inhaling water.

Frantically trying to not die, I know something is wrong when I try to use the ground below me to push upward to the surface. A force keeps me under the water and I try to see through the cloudy liquid.

My stomach drops when I realise that my long coat is caught on a massive underwater rock.

Pulling and tugging while trying to fight my instinct to take a breath, I begin to fear that this is it. That my life will end right here and everything I've worked towards, everything I've built, will be for nothing.

Mama's face flashes in my mind. The words she spoke all those years ago in her grief that gave me the power to do what needed to be done haunts my ears as I struggle to free myself.

Black spots invade my vision, making it hard to work out a plan of action. The wolf under my skin helps as best she can. The pounding in my temple has made it hard for me to connect with her. To let her take the reins and shift. She's not a great swimmer anyway but right now I could use her to get out of these clothes.

However, I can't connect with her.

Chest screaming, I try to remove the coat and then blink up at the figure that appears before me.

Male hands grip my shoulders. I can only see his outline as he swims upside down, his hands moving down my sides, my hips, my leg, and then to where the cloak is stuck.

I fight against the growing darkness and try to help the male who is clearly trying to save my life. The water is relentless though and I watch as his body is pushed back and forth like my own.

It's taking too long and I shut my burning eyes.

They fly open when a mouth closes over mine. Full, luscious lips clamp around half my face and my lungs fill with air.

Like magic, I breath, relieving the pressure.

Trying to process everything that's happening, I stare into pale, grey eyes as they bore into my own. All I can think is how captivating the odd colour is. They are intense and I seem to work out slowly that a second male is trying to communicate something with me.

I nod as best I can against the current to indicate that I understand. He's trying to tell me that he's going to push away. I make sure my mouth is shut and watch as he disappears to the surface.

I can think a little clearer while I wait for him to come back. The other male has a firm grip on my ankle and is trying to free me. A calmness settles over my soul as I watch the pair move in the water with ease and grace. That mouth attaches to mine another three times before I feel a tug and I begin to float.

With one male on either arm, drawing me to the surface, I fill my lungs when we break the water line.

My breathing is loud and I cough up water.

I'm crushed between two very solid, bare chested bodies as wave after wave hits us.

Everything is spinning, I do my best to help get us to safety but my energy is waning. The side of my head is throbbing and I can smell blood, which isn't helping. Blood has always made me queasy and with half the ocean in my stomach, I'm barely keeping the contents of it inside my body.

The current took me out further than I could comprehend and when my feet hit solid sand and the shore isn't too far, my legs collapse with the next wave that smashes our backs.

Strong arms lift me up and against a hard, warm bare chest.

My wolf and I are exhausted and with the cool air hitting every exposed inch of my skin, I don't have the energy to respond to the two males who begin to ask me if I'm all right.

Everything is fuzzy.

Everything goes black.

Chapter Ten

Nicollette in Rhiattline

Heavy lids refusing to stay open, I try to tell whoever is squeezing my head to leave me alone.

Two voices filter through the haze covering my brain and I manage to groan. The words are unfamiliar yet soothing.

'Open your eyes for us.'

I do and only because I'm unable to not comply with the sweet-covered demand of a male whose energy my wolf seems to respond to.

I blink away the blurriness in my vision and find myself laying on a soft bed looking up at white painted exposed beams just like in the pink bungalow. It isn't though. The air in the dwelling is enriched with the scent of summer and ocean and a whole lot of masculine tones.

It takes me a moment to realise that one of the males who rescued me is sitting very close to the bed, right beside my head. His strong, capable hands are doing something that has my heartrate spike and my wolf ready to react.

The voice that drew me out of the darkness speaks calmly and in a language that is so beautiful I wish that I knew what he was saying.

That's when the male with the strange grey eyes appears again in my line of sight. His focus snaps me out of the almost panic attack I was about to have. My wolf responds instantly to the vision of him.

His scent surrounds me. He smells like summer. Like home. I've never seen a male who looks as gorgeous as the one now smiling slowly down at me like he knows all the adjectives I'm using in my mind to describe him. Or the fact that all I can think about is his lips on mine, breathing life into my body underwater.

The bed dips when he sits beside me and warm fingers come up to brush the hair from my eyes. The black, curly mass must look a wreck after my earlier swim.

'You're safe with us.'

Damn me, I believe him.

His accent just adds to the allure of his masculine features. I study the strong jawline that is covered with a shadow of hair and the distinct high cheekbones. His skin is deeply tanned and has me grab my bottom lip between my teeth. His grey eyes are pale and his hair is dark brown and long on the top. It's all roughed and falling around his face like he just got out of bed. His straight nose makes him look younger than what I assume he is and the rounded, thin, black framed glasses make him beyond attractive. I've never had such a reaction to a male before and I shuffle on the bed.

'Easy there.'

'Wha...where am I and what are you doing?' I get a half smirk at my demand that does nothing to stop my heart rate from accelerating.

Attention snapping to the male at my head who begins to wipe a cool cloth over my forehead, my eyes widen.

I was wrong.

The male sitting beside me isn't the only one that makes my insides clench. The wolf shifter at my head, the one I'm hoping has some kind of medical training because I think he's tending to my injuries, removes the medical gloves on his hands and throws them on the table beside the bed.

Even sitting, I can tell that he's tall and lean. His arms are covered in black ink patterns that turn me on so hard I bite my lip to cover an embarrassing moan. His face is just as sharp as the other shifter.

The one who has appeared to have healed me is the male who pulled my coat from the rock. His eyes are a pure light lavender. They bore into mine as we stare, his hair is nearly black in colour. It's swept away from his face in an upward motion, I believe it's called the pompadour haircut and I only know this because August spent four months last year deciding on a new hairstyle and spoke about all the different trends and what they meant. I thought I wasn't listening but clearly I was, on some level.

This male makes me want to know all those things. Like what his hair style is called and the kind of product he uses. I want to understand him better. To know everything about him. His skin is so darkly tanned that I long to swipe my tongue over the ink and muscle just to see what it tastes like. I'm sure it would taste like the darkest of night, the depths of the ocean, like salt and spice and sin. The shadow on his jaw is longer than the other wolf and I find myself intrigued by the pull both of them seem to have over me.

'Going out into the water like that wasn't very smart! I need to stitch this gash on your forehead. I don't like the look of it. I'm worried about an infection. I've cleaned it as best I can,' the one that better be a healer says. There's a hardness in his tone that I don't like. He doesn't know me and he doesn't get to reprimand me.

'Excuse me?' I might be intrigued by his looks and his energy but he doesn't get to speak like that to me. Not even my brother, the Alpha of Farrowline, a male with more power than any shifter I've met, would speak to me in such a way.

'You could've died. You're lucky we were there to save you.'

I don't reply for some unknown reason. Normally, I'd tear this male apart. I put it down to the knock on my head which makes everything spin when I try to sit up.

'Don't,' the healer says, his large hand falls on my shoulder, keeping me down. I comply only because everything is all fuzzy. 'You hit your head hard. You need at least five stitches and I suspect you have a severe concussion. I want you to rest for the rest of the day. You'll stay here where we can monitor you. Now, do you consent?'

I have no idea what he's talking about. 'What?'

'You need stitches, are you happy for me to go ahead?'

Right. 'Are you qualified?'

There is a deep chuckle from the male across the room.

'Yes,' the 'supposed' healer states. He has that very bossy 'healer' tone so I believe him.

'I consent.' Then maybe I can go to sleep. My head is pounding.

I drift in and out of sleep while the healer works and then rouse when he gets up and declares that he's finished.

Not able to say anything in return, I listen and watch the pair as they get up from their respective positions. I can't help but check them out.

The one that stitched me up is just as tall as I thought he'd be. Lean, taunt muscle and thick arms. He moves to the kitchenette in the corner to wash his hands. That's when I notice all the supplies spilling out of an old-school medical bag.

The other shifter is shorter, but not by much. He's bulkier though, but again, not by much. There's a familiarity with how they move around the bungalow.

Shutting my eyes to stop the world from spinning like I'm underwater again, I fall asleep despite the unknown location and the fact that I'm alone with two dominant males.

Chapter Eleven

Present Day

'So, are we just going to stand here perving all day or should we go over and start the barbecue?'

Gilly giggles at her mate's tone and the sound really does make me smile. After everything that happened with Gilly and how low she was a few months ago, I love that she's happy. We all do. That's why, when Jax comes over, he is grinning too.

Our Gamma realises what's happening at the back of Mama's den and laughs loudly. 'Is that our lovely Luna?'

We all turn back to the adult-only show happening in Farrowline right now. Sure enough, there's Ridley, at the front of the mass of females, sitting with her legs under her body as she chats away with Luis. I can only imagine what the handsome male is saying to have her grinning like that.

Luis is a free-spirited soul who plays music and spends a great deal of time sitting out in nature just...existing. I spent many nights beside him on the sand, under the stars in Rhiattline, listening to him strum his acoustic guitar, talking about life and loss and love. His energy is so inviting and calming that you could talk with him for hours and spill your secrets without feeling awkward or self-conscious.

That was part of the problem.

Luis had a way of opening me up and digging around under the surface, which isn't something I want anyone to do. He saw parts of me that I had buried a long, long time ago. He made me long for things that I gave up. He made me…feel.

The trench is pretty deep and you can hardly see the two males. Ridley throws her head back and laughs at something Diego says to Luis. The pair start to argue and I know why she finds them so entertaining. The pair are joined in a way that goes beyond blood. They've killed together and survived together and loving me was something they did together.

I'm not even talking sex. Yes, the sex was great.

I'm referring to the way they pulled me into their world and consumed my soul. It happened so quickly, that in the beginning, I didn't realise what was happening.

When I did, well, the confusion over having feelings for two different males at the same time, and both being so insanely intense, I felt I had no choice but to leave them behind.

I left Rhiattline for a reason.

I can't forget how angry Diego was when I told them I needed to head back to Farrowline. It still baffles me that after everything they think they can come here and expect something from me.

They made it clear what they wanted. I wasn't in their decision making.

Diego is the complete opposite of Luis in every way. The male is a gifted healer, an extremely intelligent businessperson, and the one that came up with the tourist rental idea for Rhiattline to make an income.

He works hard, takes the responsibility of the leader easily, and loves to tell everyone what to do. However, like Luis, he's a lover and I fear once you're in his heart, there is no way to get out.

I made a choice. I've been making hard decisions since I was nineteen years old and I'll continue to make them.

I am a Farrow.

I don't have the luxury of living on a beach and playing in the waves for hours. I don't have the luxury of sitting around drawing while I have to help support one of the biggest packs in the country. A pack that has my name.

I never spoke any mating bond and I refuse to let these two males come into my life and disrupt everything I've created.

'What're we doing?' Dom steps up behind me. His oversized body so close that I can feel his body heat.

I keep my gaze on the digging shifters. Our Beta's body vibrates against my back with his laughter.

'Ahhh, that's the best thing I've seen all week. Is that your grandma Betsy and your mum, Gilly?'

Gilly stands on her tip toes, her eyes scanning the spectators. 'Fucking hell, it is.' She cracks up and wipes the tears from her face. Oliver has a dopey look on his as he watches his mate enjoy what's going on.

Me on the other hand, could really use one of those shovels to dig myself a hole so I can bury myself in it.

'Is that Ridley?' Dom asks and it's hard not to miss the pure pleasure and humour. His laughter is infectious and now everyone in this little group is laughing.

'What's going on?'

I roll my eyes and sigh at having another shifter here to watch the show. Delfina saunters up beside me and narrows her eyes at the scene.

The female's energy is always hard to read and I wonder for a moment if she's annoyed by the situation, but then she smiles slowly and deviously. She throws Dom a saucy look over her shoulder and then begins to move as if going to join the crowd.

'Hey!' Dom shouts and the big wolf pushes past me to grab his mate's arm. She turns into his chest and wraps her arms around our Beta's neck, giggling like an adolescent. 'The only male you'll be watching dig a hole is me, little wolf.'

'Yeah?' she all but purrs. 'Doesn't matter anyway, I was here about half an hour ago with Mama, so I've seen the show,' Delfina says it so seriously that it takes everyone a moment to process what she's just said.

Jax bursts into fits of laughter.

Gilly can't breathe she is laughing so hard and Dom growls so loudly that even I laugh despite the situation.

Dom and Delfina share a passionate kiss and then stop and pull away when a massive shadow falls on us all.

Chapter Twelve

Present Day

'What's going on here?'

Everyone moves out of the way to let the Alpha through. When he stands beside me, I push off the wall. My brother looks down at me approvingly as if telling me that he's happy I listened to his instructions to come back to pack, it just annoys me.

I didn't come here because of him. I came because I have a responsibility to fix this mess and I'm not a female who shies away from her problems.

My brother has no idea that everyone is smirking behind his back and waiting for his reaction as he stares at what's happening at the back of our mother's den.

One eyebrow raised over those green, family eyes, Tobias assesses the situation and locks his gaze squarely on the human having a great time with our guests.

I know how he's going to react before he does, with a small shake of his head and an exasperated sigh. It's how our father would've reacted. Mated pairs are for life. They're soul bound. Equals. There is no jealousy.

Tobias makes sure to give all of us a reprimanding look before giving me his full attention. 'Why are you over here when your mates are over there distracting half the pack, including my mate?'

Jax chuckles and I hope he gets the full meaning of my glare when I throw one at him over Tobias's shoulder.

'Can you not call them my mates?'

'But they are, aren't they?' Dom asks, his arm is draped over Delfina's shoulders and there's a look in her eye as she stares at me, like she is making sure that I'm all right.

'Were they unkind to you? Is that why you left them behind?' she asks and the change in the males around me is instant. 'Because I will go over there and rip their throats out.' She really would.

There's a collective low growl as the Circle of Farrowline look over at the digging males and I swear Diego's shoulders stiffen as if he's listening to everything we're saying. Which he probably is, he's a very powerful dominant. He could match any of the energies of the ones standing around me right now.

'No, relax!' I command softly. Such dramatics. 'As if I'd let any male treat me in any way that I didn't see as appropriate.'

That seems to calm them all down.

'True,' Jax states, completely at ease again.

They know me. We've known each other our entire lives.

Well, except Delfina, but she has embedded herself so far into our pack that it's like she has always been around. I don't blame her for thinking that I might have left because of that. Her birthpack are full of complete arseholes. Dom plants a kiss on her head and the smaller wolf leans into it.

'So...' Gilly draws out the word before saying, 'why are you standing over here when those two attractive males are over there digging a hole for your mum?'

'*Very* attractive,' Jax adds as if he's agreeing with her and gets a solid grin from Gilly that has him flex his muscles. Damn fool.

'You know you can all go away, yes? I didn't ask any of you to come over here and stand with me. I don't need your support. You're all welcome to go over there and begin the barbecue for our dinner.' I can't help my tone.

Secretly, I want to get back in my car and drive to the office and finish my work. I have about a thousand emails to get to, and now that I have two charity dinners lined up, I'll need to make some appointments to the local designers to get outfits.

I will not let August pick something for me this time. The last event I was showing half my back in a form-fitting shimmering slip of cloth that I hated.

'We know you don't need our help Nic. You've been taking care of yourself and the pack since you were young,' Dom states casually.

'But here we stand. With you. Making sure that you're all right before you walk over there and become the centre of attention,' Jax says.

'We all know how much you *love* being the centre of attention,' Gilly finishes. While I want to smack them all, I also love them dearly, so I just ignore it.

'I'm too busy for this.' I sigh, knowing there's no way out of going over there and speaking to Luis and Diego.

Tobias pats me on the back for encouragement. 'We're all busy Nicolette.' I know he's teasing.

'Well, Ridley looks really busy,' Dom jokes and has everyone laughing again.

Mumbling my annoyance, I walk away from the teasing and growling.

I really hope that no one notices that I go into the den and not toward the 'situation' I need to handle. I just need time to think.

I just need…time.

Chapter Thirteen

Present Day

Laptop open and headphones in my ear, I dive into the issue August has just rung me about. Damn interns sent the wrong contracts to an important client. I now have a very aggressive email from a man who needs to remember who he is speaking to.

'I'm sorry, Nicolette, I should've checked.'

'I'll fix it. Mr Prescott is a cranky bastard on the best of days so this is just another excuse for him to be a prick. He thinks that because of my age and my female parts, I'm here for him to reprimand and give a hard time to.'

'Poor man has no idea who he's dealing with.'

'No, I think he's forgotten, which is why I'm sending him an email right now cancelling his contract and sending him to Oliver so that he can deal with our legal team.'

August whistles in appreciation. 'Damn, I love working for you, Nicolette Farrow. You're my spirit animal.'

Head shaking and grinning down at my laptop, I finish up my assertive email and send it off to Mr Prescott with a satisfying click. No male, human or shifter, writes an email like that to me because of an error made by an intern. I'm sure Tobias is going to come storming into the back living room at Mama's den, where I'm *not* hiding, to ask me to explain why he's got a phone call from Mr Prescott.

'Shouldn't you be at a pack barbecue?'

'I am,' I reply to the male still talking in my ear.

'You're probably sitting in a corner somewhere, happy that this work issue has come up so you can use it as an excuse to not deal with those hunky males.'

'Goodbye August,' I snap and hang up.

Pulling the device out of my ear, I place it next to my phone on the coffee table and get to some of the other emails and tasks while I'm here in the quiet. The pack is loud and enjoying the meal I can smell wafting through the den.

No one will come back here, not when Jax and Oliver are cooking. They're the masters. The food in Farrowline is always amazing so everyone is enjoying the fun.

Well, everyone except Mama who appears from down the hall and sits in the armchair across from me.

I don't look up. 'I'll come and eat in a moment,' I tell her while typing.

'Good,' she answers calmly and I look up at her over my laptop screen. She has that tone. The one that tells me that she's disappointed or upset with me.

'Mum, I'll come outside when I'm done fixing this issue.'

Nodding, Mama doesn't look too impressed. 'But there's always an issue, Nicolette. Work can't be the priority, sweetheart. Especially when you have two males out there who are wooing the entire pack and speaking about you like you're the centre of their universe. Like they only breathe because of you.'

I bristle. Shuffling on the couch, I try to ignore her. She keeps going as if she has no idea what her words do to me. She doesn't know what happened between me, Diego and Luis. Now, I'm starting to worry about what they're saying out there.

'I don't know why it's so hard for you to accept the gift of two mates, honey. I don't know if I've done something as a parent, or if losing your father —'

'Don't,' I say a little too roughly and watch as my mum closes her mouth. I feel instantly bad.

'Nicolette, when are you going to stop punishing yourself for what happened? I miss your father too. Every day is hard, but you have to move forward with your life. I see what you do. I know why you do it. And I can't let you continue to hide behind your work.'

I snap. The leash over my anger cracks and I can't keep my retort inside. 'What would you have me do then, Mum? I'm a Farrow and it's my job to contribute to pack like it is for Tobias, and for you. I have a job here and playing mate isn't going to help anyone. I know what my role is. Why do you all think that you can come at me about how I support the pack?'

I keep what I really want to say to myself. I keep that I heard her in the early days of my father's passing and that I'm very aware how hard it is for my mum and how my responsibilities extend beyond financially supporting Farrowline.

'Then become a Circle member, Nicolette!' Mama retorts. 'Pledge your full loyalty to your brother through the promise of living here in Farrowline forever!'

My jaw hits my lap. I've never heard my mum be so harshly. I don't want to be a Circle member and she knows that.

'So what, everything I do for this pack isn't good enough? The funds I bring in to support everyone, isn't good enough? You want my blood too?' I can't believe what I'm hearing. *It's never enough.*

'No honey, what I'm saying is that deep down you know there's more to life and more to what you're supposed to do than commit your entire existence to your birth-pack. This is not who you are, or who you were destined to be, Nicolette.'

My mind is reeling. I think I misinterpret everything Mama is saying and it's hurting my soul. She's being harsh and I don't know why.

'I do all of this for you,' I state firmly, hoping she can see the sincerity in my gaze as we stare.

I don't look much like Mama. I inherited my honey coloured eyes from my dad. The black curls on my head are my mum's though. My lean build is all to do with me being a dominant. Over the years I've been told that my attitude is all my dad's. It's a compliment even when it wasn't always said as one.

'I know Nicolette. I'm sorry. I'm not your responsibility. You're *mine.*'

I just sit, staring at the wall. She can say those words all she wants but that doesn't make it true.

Mama walks out of the loungeroom with a quick demand that I come and eat and stop ignoring my mates.

I can't find the energy to get up and follow her, not when our conversation has stirred up memories that I've tried to bury.

Chapter Fourteen

Nicolette is Nineteen

'No! You will *not* leave me behind Tobias!' I shout, enraged at what's happening right now. I'm standing in the doorway to the den, hands on hips, furious and nearly in tears.

'Just relax, Nicolette. We aren't going anywhere.'

Tobias is lying. I can tell by the hard set of his jaw and the look in his eyes.

'Bullshit! I know what you're doing and you *will* take me with you!' I can't control myself. I'm yelling. I just can't believe that they think that they can leave without me.

'Nicolette, you can't come with us,' Dominic says with that damn sympathetic tone I haven't stopped hearing.

Oliver and Jax are both nodding like they're all for me staying out of their plans for revenge.

Poking Dominic in the chest, I remind him that he can't tell me what to do.

Arms up defensively, Dom just glances at Tobias over my head as if waiting for him to control his errant, hysterical sister.

'Nicolette, I need you to move out of the way.'

I use my body to block the door more and watch as Tobias rolls his eyes. The grief lines on his face match my own.

'Nic, you need to stay here with Sara and Mama and make sure they're okay,' Liam tells me sweetly, always trying to be the diplomat of the group.

'*You* stay here with them!' I demand, hurting his feelings, but I couldn't care less. This is important to me. This affected me too.

The death of my father is something I have the right to avenge.

Tobias grips my shoulders, forcing me to look at him and I hate the hardness on his face. I hate the way the wolf under my skin recognises his Alpha energy and that I know deep down that whatever he says now I'll follow because I have to. He is my alpha. And it hurts.

'Nicolette, you will stay in den. We'll be back soon.'

Lip wobbling, I refuse to cry. I haven't cried in front of anyone yet because no one needs my tears.

They're useless and unhelpful. I leave them for late at night once I know Mum and Sara are in bed, fed and sleeping.

The pair take up all of my time. I know Tobias is busy. The entire pack, hundreds of wolf shifters, are now under his care, but I wish some nights he'd come over and take the burden from me. Just to give me a break. To act like *my* alpha.

'I'm angry too, Tobias. He was my dad too. I deserve to come with you. I'm just as dominant as any of you and I won't be sidelined because you think I can't handle whatever it is you're going to do. Vestraline will pay for what they did! I'm coming!'

Green eyes hardening, Tobias doesn't drop his hands from my shoulders. 'Nic, I need you to stay here and look after the pack. If something happens, you are a Farrow and Mum and Sara aren't in any state to be left with the responsibility.'

His words hit so hard it hurts. I've lost my dad and the idea that I could lose Tobias or any of these males it's too much to bear.

The selfishness of what he is asking is unfathomable. *Does he not see how much pain I'm in? Does he not care?*

'You can't ask me to do that.'

'But I have to, because we all have a role to play now to keep Farrowline safe and thriving. We all have a responsibility. You. Me. Dom. All of us.' He indicates to the males around him.

Dominic. Oliver. Jax. Liam. Easton.

Tobias's Circle now that he's the Alpha of Farrowline.

Now that our father is gone.

Tobias named Dominic his Beta the same day we lost Dad and then the entire Pack watched as one-by-one the last four males took the blood bond.

'Please, Nicolette. I need you to help me with pack. I need you to be a Farrow.'

I almost flinch. It's so close to what Dad said to me the day he was murdered that it opens the wound of his death wider.

I bleed internally. The pain is hard to function through.

Nodding once, I understand what I need to do. I have no power to fight with my new Alpha. The wolf under my skin won't let me even though the human side of my soul is raging like a bull in a pen.

I watch as my brother and the males who'll help run this pack leave Mama's den with a look of determination and fury.

They haven't openly said what they're going to do tonight but everyone knows. That's why a line of dominants are standing in the front yard, each of them falling into step behind the Alpha of Farrowline, to seek justice for what happened.

Closing the door gently, I walk on silent, bare feet to the wing of my mother's den where her and Sara's bedrooms are. I can hear the steady breathing coming from my sister's room and know that she's asleep.

Liam stays with her every night now. He sleeps above the covers holding her as she falls asleep, it's the only way we can get her to stop crying and rest. I hope that my dad was right about the two of them because I fear Liam is now stuck within Sara's night-time routine.

Moving quietly down the hall, I stop just shy of Mama's door when voices drift down the den.

Chapter Fifteen

Nicolette is Nineteen

My mother's tears are never ending. Our healer has already been in today and gave her some fluids and a sleeping mixture to help her relax enough to rest.

I'm sceptical though. My mother has lost the life in her eyes. I know what they say about mated females and males who lose their partners. Most just drift off into the next life, unable to handle the loss. They close their eyes and follow their mates.

They let go.

Others stay for their pups until they know that they're looked after and secure enough before they follow their waiting soulmate.

The thought of losing Mum has me lean against the wall, breathing unsteadily, listening to her speak to Maree.

My heart is broken. The shattered pieces now tiny shards that I fear will never be placed back together.

'I don't know how to live without him, Maree. It's too much. It hurts too much.' Mum's tone is one of someone utterly devastated.

I know everyone is worried about her, about the future of Farrowline. We can't lose Mama, not now, not when we're grieving a loss so unimaginable that the ceremony we had last week for our fallen packmates ended with every wolf shifter, from the elderly to the very young, on their knees, silently grieving those who were taken from us.

'I know, sweetheart. I know.' Maree is barely holding back her tears. You can hear it in her voice.

She has been a great help these last two weeks which I guess she can be. Her mate survived the attack on my father and his Circle. The male is barely keeping it together himself. Maree has been fussing constantly.

I feel instantly bad for thinking that. I actually don't know what I'd do without her. I didn't even hear her enter the den which is the concerning part. I was so focused on Tobias that I wasn't aware of what was happening in our den. I guess that wasn't really my job before now.

My dad was here monitoring things like that. I spent my entire life knowing that he was around to protect us, to know what was happening and to monitor our den and pack.

Now...

I slide down the wall until my butt hits the floor. Now, it's my job to make sure that Mama and Sara are taken care of. That the pack is taken care of.

Gripping my chest, in fear of the pain radiating through my heart, I bite my lip to keep from crying out with the agony of listening to my mum say the next few words to Maree.

'I don't know if I can do this, Maree. I don't think I can bear it.'

'You have to! You have three pups who need their mother. Sara is too young to lose you. Tobias needs guidance. He has been thrown into the deep end and is now the Alpha, and Nicolette...' I don't catch what Maree says about me over Mama's wailing.

'I know,' she cries. 'I'll find my strength, Maree. I will, eventually. I won't follow Caleb until all my pups are happy and secure, but I need to find the energy to keep going. I'm afraid to even try to carry on without him.'

Tears leak down my face at her words. My mum is broken and I don't have the tools to fix her.

'I hated him when I first met him,' Mum chuckles softly, there's longing in her voice.

'I know. Caleb was a bit of a dick, wasn't he?'

Mama laughs and it's music to my ears. I've heard this story so many times. The early years of my parents story is funny and ridiculous and kinda like a fairy-tale. My parents hated each other in the beginning, but when they eventually fell in love, they fell hard, and their devotion created a den full of joy and love. There are so many memories of Sara, Tobias and I groaning around the dinner table when Mum and Dad would start reminiscing on their youthful tales. We secretly loved hearing it even though we gave them hell for being so 'uncool'. I'd give anything to go back to those moments.

Anything.

'He saved my life,' Mama says. 'I wouldn't be here if it wasn't for him.'

'And he'd want you to be strong now for the Pack,' Maree finishes.

There are a few noises behind the door like someone is tidying up.

'I will be. For my pups. Until I know that they're okay.'

I can't hear the rest of what is said. All I know is that no matter how selfish it makes me, I'll make sure that my mum understands that she's needed so that we can keep her here longer. Whatever it takes. Even if I have to live without a mate and never be happy, or if I have to work hard and pick up the burden of caring for my family and our Pack, then that's what I'll do.

Until my day comes when I will see my father again, I'll make sure that Mum knows she's needed and loved.

No matter what it takes from me.

Chapter Sixteen

Present Day

It's the music that has me eventually leave the front room and face my problems. The voice that flows through the den draws me out to the back patio. It pulls at my soul. Memories flood my mind of sitting on the sand with the stars blinking overhead, the waves crashing in the background, with my gaze locked on the male playing his guitar and singing for me.

The power of my emotions has me stop at the railing and grip the hard wood as I take in the scene of Mama's backyard. Farrowline is dancing. Couples embrace as they sway to the mesmerising voice that takes up every single cell in my body. Ridley and Tobias are in their own little world, gazing into each other's eyes while the rest of the Circle laugh and dance together with their females.

It's a beautiful scene that shouldn't make me sad, and yet, I hold back tears with the sheer force of my stubbornness.

Across the grass, sitting on a long table, with his leg propped on the back of the chair so he can hold his acoustic guitar to his chest, Luis sits like temptation sent from hell to torment me. He's gorgeous. That face. The glasses. The lazy smile as he absorbs the joy his music is giving everyone. The auror of calm and kindness. He is the complete package.

His voice is a gift from the heavens. It's smooth and deep and intoxicating. Each word Luis sings is like hearing the voice of an angel. He sings in the language of his birth-pack. It doesn't matter that I can't understand the words, they hypnotise my soul. I know he sings of passion and love and action because that is what Luis is. He is what he sings. He is how he sings. He is a lover. A protector. He was all mine for a moment in time until I gave it all up.

The last words we spoke to each other were cruel and harsh and they broke me. I've been finding it hard to breath since the day I left Rhiattline. Since the day I chose my Pack, my job, and my responsibilities over my heart. It has been months and I actually thought that they'd let me go. I believed that I ruined us.

How stupid I was to think that these males would let me leave.

Luis hits the middle chorus and looks up to catch me staring. Our eyes lock and I'm hit with an overwhelming need to run to him. To wrap my arms around his solid frame and ask him to not let go. My wolf whimpers under my skin, begging me to let her go to him.

Luis's smile drops as we continue to stare and I see the hurt from our last encounter. I see the longing I feel in my own heart and I see the offer he made all those weeks ago that I couldn't accept.

They just didn't understand and that was the problem. They wanted too much. They asked for too much.

I couldn't give it to them and I had to make a choice.

I follow Luis' gaze, knowing who it'll lead me to. How can I not? I'm fully aware of them, like a cord linking me to the pair that I don't think even death would be able to sever. I'd find them anywhere in the world.

Diego is dancing with Mama and I quickly wipe the tear that escapes down my cheek at the sight of the tall, gorgeous male spinning my laughing mother around. She seems so happy and I don't blame her. Being inside Diego's tattooed embrace is like finding home.

The song comes to a melodic end just as Diego looks over at Luis as if he can sense that he's staring at him, another example of their ability to read each other's mind. I'm sure it is a superpower they both have that they continue to deny. Then both their attention moves slowly away from each other and I'm met with the unmistakable force of their combined gaze.

The absence of music, and the emotions that move between us, brings me back to reality. I genuinely don't know why they're both here. While I've hated being away from them, I left for a reason. Our fight all those weeks ago has me steel my spin and remember who I am.

The illusion of the moment shatters around me.

Turning my back, I head inside knowing that they will follow.

Chapter Seventeen

Present Day

Arms folded, foot tapping, I lean against the door with my arms over my chest, enraged at the situation. I headed straight for my room at the back of Mama's den and was followed.

Now, I refuse to enter my personal space with Luis and Diego in the room, looking around. Touching my things. Marking their scent throughout the place like they have the right to. I know what they're doing, I grew up with Tobias, Dom, Oliver and Liam. I'm very aware of the behaviour of dominant wolf shifter males. They're doing it on purpose.

I refuse to let the 'Luis-Diego affect' draw me under their spell again. It did back in Rhiattline where I stupidly let my guard down and allowed myself to enjoy my holiday.

'I'm not doing this!' I state firmly.

'I don't think you have much of a choice, cónyuge,' Luis replies smoothly, his focus on the pile of forms on my desk. It's a massive room. Big king bed in the middle, a full wardrobe behind the wall it sits against.

A decent sized bathroom is behind the door to the right. Mum decorated the place when I was a teen. It's all whites and greys. My time is normally split between here and the office. Mostly the office.

'Don't call me that!' I know what that means. Cónyuge. It means spouse. Mate.

'But it is what you are,' Diego is the one to reply. I don't appreciate his tone. It's so...male. Why am I so concerned that he sounds just as angry as me! They don't get to be angry. They're the ones that told me to pick. They're the ones that gave me the ultimatum, which I didn't appreciate.

'I never accepted anything! I never voiced the bond.' My words hang between us and I refuse to take a step back when both males look over at me. Luis just frowns and Diego gives me a look like I'm somehow unintelligent and naive.

'I don't think it matters after the bonds we formed, Nicolette.'

I have no reply. There is a part, deep down— like deep, deep down— that knows he's right.

That doesn't mean that I accept what he's saying.

'Why are you both here? You made it very clear that me leaving Rhiattline was the end of us.' The more I say, the angrier I get. 'You both questioned my loyalty and I told you that I wouldn't leave Farrowline or my responsibilities to play mate in your bungalow.'

Neither of them react. They just sit on different sides of the room. Diego gracefully lowers himself in the chair by my dresser table. Luis finds a spot on the long chest at the end of the bed. The wooden box was carved by my father. The flowery details and the little messages engraved around the sides would captivate my attention as a pup. I've traced every pattern and words so many times in my life that I think I could recreate the entire box just off memory alone. There should actually be an entire sketchbook somewhere in storage with countless drawings where I added my own elements to the wood in my imagination.

That sketchbook is packed up now.

'Nicolette, what was said was done in anger and passion. Neither Diego or I meant it, and we are sorry. We tried to reach out to you to say that, but you have ignored every attempt we made.' Luis is so calm while I'm seething and huffing like an adolescent who can't control her emotions.

'He never contacted me!' I point to Diego. The arrogant ass sits in my chair looking at me like I'm the problem. 'It's been months,' I snap back, unsure if they hear the subtle hurt in my tone. I didn't mean for it to slip through and stand still, hoping that they didn't catch it.

Diego isn't looking at the mass of jewellery and products on my dresser any longer. His lavender eyes are fixed on me and I can't help but stare back.

'You know we had to stay with Gloria after what happened. She needed us. We couldn't leave my sister. Did you not understand that?' Diego retorts, and I want to smack him. He clearly hasn't changed.

The thing is, I did understand. Gloria, the reason Diego and Luis were staying in Rhiattline, had a fall not long after her mating ceremony that left her bed-bound.

Unfortunately, Gloria was patrolling within the inner territory and broke her hip. It was terrible. I remember waking to Diego shouting at his sisters new mate on the phone. Luis was still beside me in the bed and I'll never forget the worry lines that marked his face. She needed surgery, and Diego being Diego, refused to let anyone touch his sister without him being present. He worked closely with the human surgeons outside the pack and assisted in the surgery. It was hard on the poor female. While she was young, the entire ordeal affected her both physically and mentally.

I left the night of her operation. My holiday was over, Tobias needed me back in pack. Luis and Diego didn't agree or approve. They couldn't understand what I was thinking even though the night before they informed me that they were moving to Claymore after Diego received a job offer. They hadn't included me in that decision! Yet, they were angry when I left.

'Yes, I understood. I understood exactly what was going on, Diego. It was you and Luis who didn't understand. We had a beautiful time together. It was not a commitment. I can't give you what you want. I have responsibilities here that I can't turn my back on.'

The silence that fills the space is weighted and full of tension. Luis and Diego stare for a long time before the pair rise to their feet, in unison.

'We'll leave you to your sleep. You'll have a busy day tomorrow, I'm sure. Your work is important.'

Like I've been slapped, I flinch at the harsh tone of Diego's voice.

Luis looks sad, his hair falling around his face. I have an overwhelming need to go to him and lick his deeply tanned skin, knowing exactly what it would taste like. My damn wolf makes a deep noise in my throat that I shut down immediately.

Luis strides lazily towards me. I want him to touch me. I want him to caress my cheek like he used to do back in the bungalow we shared. Every time he walked past he would touch me in some way.

'Your bedroom has no soul, bonita. This place is not you. There is no art. No passion. No, Nicolette.'

Taken aback, I find my jaw drop. His words hurt more than what Diego has just said.

As if he knows the way his assessment of my room hit, Luis' grey eyes soften slightly. 'Your mother has offered us rooms that I believe are down the hall. Diego and I will stay there. We have permission from your Alpha to remain in Farrowline for a few days. If you need us, we will come.'

Luis walks past me and out into the hall without a touch. I almost grab him, just to feel his skin on mine.

Balling my hands into fists at my side, I draw my attention to the male who walks after him. Diego says nothing and it's almost worse than Luis telling me my private space has no life.

I watch, knowing the exact rooms Mama would have put the pair. They are down the hall that leads to the main part of the house. Directly across from each other.

My phone buzzes in my back pocket and pushing aside all the useless worries and fears, I pull it out and get to work fixing the fall-out of the contract I just terminated.

Chapter Eighteen

Nicolette in Rhiattline

I wake up to my head pounding and my stomach growling. Feeling groggy and a little queasy, I roll over, ignoring the pain in my head and blink up at the arched ceiling.

Everything comes back slowly but no less intensely. I nearly drowned because I was too busy being annoyed at Mum and not paying attention to what I was doing. It was stupid.

Turning to the device on the bedside that begins to vibrate dramatically on the hard surface, I groan softly as I try to reach over and grab it.

'Easy there, bonita.' A smooth voice catches my attention and I stare, almost stunned at the male who appears beside me. I watch silently as he reaches out and grabs my phone. Handing it to me, the male smiles and I try to process if I actually did die in that water. He's stunning and then, I remember the pair of wolf shifters that saved me and…touching my forehead gently, I feel the bandage that has been taped against my skin.

'You must be a very important female. This thing hasn't stopped making noise.'

I don't know what it means that my wolf is so calm or that she even allowed me to sleep here.

I can't scent the other male, the tattooed one that stitched me up. Shuffling over a little, I feel like I should be demanding that he back away or insist that he tells me who he is and where I am. Instead, I stay quiet and let him sit beside me.

'I hope you don't mind that I put your phone on silent so that you could rest. Diego said that you needed to sleep to recover. He was very worried about how hard you hit your head.' His slight accent is intoxicating and is all I can focus on as I lie here, in a very submissive position. It's just…I don't think I've felt this calm in a very long time. I don't know if it's his scent or if it's the shock at how unbelievably attractive he is, which is not like me at all.

Maybe I did hit my head too hard.

'Where am I?' I manage to say, getting a hold of myself.

'You're in Diego's bungalow. We're staying here in Rhiattline while his sister gets settled. I'm guessing you're with one of the many groups that've come to this pack for the mating ceremony.'

'Diego?' I feel like I'm starting a movie halfway through.

The male chuckles slightly and I can imagine it's because of the confused look on my face. 'Let's slow this down.' He grins reassuringly at me. 'My name is Luis Cortez, originally from the Pack of Riveraline.' He interprets my small frown and explains further for me. 'I'm not from these lands. My birth-pack was from across the seas and in an unstable country where packs fight for leadership and land, to the death. My brother, in every way but blood, and his sister and I have been on our own for many years. Recently, Gloria found her mate while studying here in this country, and here we are.' His voice is mesmerising. 'So, that is my little life story, bonita.'

'You called me that before, what does it mean?'

'It means beautiful girl.' Damn, I feel the colour rise to my cheeks. I'm blushing and his big, boyish grin lights his face. He has the most inviting lips. Kissable. *I did hit my head too hard.* 'I'll make you some breakfast and then you can explain to me why you were swimming fully clothed during the off season when these waters are dangerous.'

Luis gets up and moves around the bungalow and I feel like I'm able to find my equilibrium without his attention on me. For a moment there I felt like an infatuated adolescent and not the very powerful, wealthy and successful female that I am.

Sitting up, I push aside the sense of vertigo and check my phone with a sigh. So many notifications.

Getting to work replying to August, I give him a run-down of everything I need him to do and let him know that I'll call later tonight. I leave out the incident and the males. I don't need August on my case.

I start getting really annoyed though because I keep mis-spelling words and forgetting what I need to write half-way through a sentence. Ignoring the pain in my head that's making it hard for me to see, I continue to try and push through it.

Head snapping up from my phone when my wolf alerts me to a new scent, I gape at the face looking down at me.

Diego.

His lavender eyes are definitely not something that I imagined, they're odd and captivating. His lean, muscular form screams dominant shifter. 'You have a severe concussion. This,' the males says, taking the liberty of grabbing the phone from my hand, 'is banned.'

I open and close my mouth a few times as the words I want to shout back at him slip through my fog covered mind. I seem to remember the word I want to call him and then lose it instantly.

'Exactly,' he states like he has proved some kind of point.

I have no idea what he's going on about. 'What?'

Diego places my phone in his back pocket, keeping those disarmingly beautiful eyes on me. 'That thing never stops. Who is August?'

I open and close my mouth three times before I can actually answer. I don't feel very well. 'What?' is all I come up with. My head is killing me.

I watch as one eyebrow rises, causing lines to appear on his masculine face. His skin is the same deep tan as Luis, yet, unlike Luis, Diego seems all hard lines and take-command energy. He starts moving around the bed and then he's at my head, touching my bandage. 'Are you in pain?'

I go to tell him I'm fine because I really don't want him to be this close to me and then snap it shut when Diego's deep voice warns that I shouldn't lie to a healer. Luis's laughter filters from the kitchenette.

I contemplate how best to respond but my upbringing gets in the way of me giving him a piece of my mind. Not that I remember what I should say, because again, my words have left me. All I croak out is, 'my head hurts.'

Nodding, Diego gets to work fiddling with a bag sitting on the bedside table. My entire body tenses when I see the syringe he pulls out. 'What are you doing?'

Lavender eyes settle on me and the hardness around them seems to soften at whatever the healer sees on my face. 'I'm going to give you an injection to help with the pain, and then you can sleep. Rest and recovery is what you need.'

My heart is in my throat and I feel the skin on my arm ripple as my wolf responds to my panic at seeing the needle.

Diego frowns deeply before he seems to realise what I'm staring at. He examines the needle in his hand and then grunts a noise. 'There is no need for your wolf to come out and play, yet. This won't hurt, I promise.'

His words don't really make sense and then Luis is beside me, sitting on the bed. He takes my hand in his and I instantly relax. My wolf retreats. I'm so freakin' confused.

'I hate needles too. Damn things always hurt, even when they tell you it doesn't. It's okay to be afraid, you can hold onto my hand.'

'I'm not afraid,' are the stupid, proud words that come from my mouth. I regret them instantly.

Luis smirks and it's more like a predator whose found a prey to target then in humour. 'I know, but I'd like to hold your hand anyway, if you'd allow me?'

The males share a look I can't decipher and I nod slowly to Luis' request.

I don't watch the needle as it goes in, I just have eyes for Luis and he seems to love the attention. Diego tells me everything he is doing before he does it and I barely feel the thing as it goes in.

'Rest. You're under our care now, Nicolette Farrow.'

Why does every word sound like a warning and a promise at the same time?

My heart does a weird flutter in my chest. A warmth flows through my veins and I lay back against the pillow. The pain relief is instant and I have no power to lift my lids as I drift off to sleep.

Chapter Nineteen

Present Day

'Just get it all sorted and tell Monica that I trust her to pick a few dresses and just send them the office. No August! I don't want you to pick my dress for the event. Let the designer do her job and you finish getting the McGrath contract sent to me immediately. Because you're banned remember?'

Fiddling with the coffee machine on the counter, I try to get the damn thing to work. It's too early and I need my caffeine fix before Mama's 'guests' wake up and demand we talk more.

After last night's conversation, I tossed and turned all night and *not* because I couldn't stop thinking about them both, sleeping naked, only a few feet away from me. No, that was definitely not what I was doing at all. It was because what they both said was harsh. Luis hated my bedroom and Diego, well, he didn't say a thing.

At least I can always rely on the bear shifter having a go at me in my ear about how unfairly I treat him.

I smile and only because my assistant isn't in the same room as me. His voice has risen an octave as he demands that I accept that his taste in clothing is impeccable. 'Debatable,' I add when he stops ranting. 'Now, send a reminder to the heads of Farrow Group about the meeting this afternoon. We need to run through some details as we lead into the coming financial year. I'll be in the office after lunch.' I feel the presence of the two males who enter the living space and add, 'I have some things to deal with here.'

'It's always a *pleasure* speaking to you, Ms Farrow,' is the last thing August says, in the sassiest tone imaginable, before he hangs up. Such a pup. He'll sook for days now that I've refused to let him help me pick my dresses for the upcoming functions. *I'm definitely firing him today.*

'I hope I get to meet your August while we're here. I know his voice so well.' I note the sarcasm and the slight hint of jealousy in Diego's tone.

Turning from my failed attempt to get the coffee grinder piece out of the holder, I lock eyes with the male daring to challenge me this early in the morning. 'Diego, I don't have the time or the patience for whatever this is. Nor do I need to hear how you don't understand my work or my responsibilities.' Hands on hips, I glare at the gorgeous male, refusing to give into the need to drop to my knees and beg him to take me. The male is standing near the hallway to our rooms with nothing more than a pair of loose dark grey trackpants that sit very low on his hips. He's playing dirty and I swallow the next words that try to escape my lips. My wolf whines. My mouth fills with saliva. I want a taste so bad that I have to clench my fists to use my nails to ground myself.

Diego knows exactly what he's doing because he saunters into the living space and comes right up to the kitchen counter across from me. 'I never said I don't understand your responsibilities, amor. I just said that you do too much at your own expense. That is what I don't agree with.'

I glare at the way he calls me '*love*'. 'I don't need you to agree with anything.'

Great, why do I sound so petulant?

Luis breezes into the kitchen and walks behind me, his hand comes up to brush against the side of my cheek, making me forget my anger at the male watching me closely. Luis isn't looking at me though, he's staring at Diego, 'come on, mi hermano. You know how our Nicolette gets when she hasn't had her coffee. Let her wake up before we demand she accept this and we can all live happily ever after.'

Too lost in the emotions that wrap around my heart whenever I hear the pair refer to each other as bothers, I miss most of what he says next. *Mi hermano, my brother.* After the long nights hearing of the suffering these two have shared, the words have such a deeper meaning for them. They don't say brother in the sense of blood, or even refer to each other as packmates, it's more than that. It's a connection that I was so afraid to ruin with my feelings for them both. When things started heating up between us all, I was always worried to get in the way. That jealousy would ruin their relationship. Which was the last thing I ever wanted.

It didn't though. It strengthened it.

But we aren't mates! I didn't voice a thing. I can't be with them. They're too free. Too committed to a life moving around and exploring. I need to be in Farrowline.

I don't process what Luis has just said until he's handing me a freshly made coffee.

'What does *demand she accepts this* mean?' I challenge. It's a total delayed reaction. The pair ignore me and sit at the long dining table.

'What does what mean?' Mama asks, coming through the den. I almost groan at the sight of her. I use my coffee cup to hide my eye roll. Mum has made an effort this morning to look presentable. She has her hair all done up and a touch of blush on her cheeks. Unlike me with my cream striped pyjama bottoms that are two sizes too big, a ribbed white tee and my hair a mass of undefined curls. This is how we normally come to breakfast, not look like we've been up for an hour getting ready.

Diego and Luis spring off their seats at Mum's appearance and head straight for her. She beams as they both kiss a cheek each and they help lead her to the table. I don't know where Diego got the shirt from but he's no longer topless and I wouldn't put it past the male to have had his tee stuffed in his back pocket just to get a rise out of me.

Luis holds out Mama's chair while Diego enquires about how my mother feels this morning. It's kind of an odd question but before I can ask, the back door is pulled open and my morning goes from bad to worse.

A line of shifters enter the den. The noise amps up with Jax's booming laughter and Noah squealing as he rides the big Gamma's shoulders.

Diego and Luis are on their feet again and I quickly check to see how they're reacting to the line of males and females who are clearly here to see them.

I don't know why I was worried because the moment the horde enter, they're greeting everyone like they live here.

I don't know how it makes me feel really and remind myself that they were here for three days while I was staying at the office.

Tobias is the last to walk in with Adalee. He's carrying an armful of bags and I pep up at the thought of Adalee's cooking.

Easton hovers close as his mate greets Luis as if they're old friends and I'm sure they have become close. Luis loves to cook and he's very gifted.

Food is the only reason I find a spot at the table.

Chapter Twenty

Present Day

Sitting around the table, the conversation ebbs and flows while I pick at my food and read the message August just sent me about a meeting clash this afternoon. I try to stay present in the big 'happy' pack breakfast but watching Diego and Luis integrate themselves perfectly into my world is making me feel...too much.

Family and pack means a great deal to the pair and that reflects in the way they treat the females at the table, my sister and Mama in particular, and how Luis refuses to give up Gianna, my niece, who he hasn't stopped cuddling since the pup woke from her carrier. It says a great deal that Liam seems perfectly content with the new male holding her.

'So Diego, Kieran told me how happy he is to have you here and that you were an exceptional help in the pack clinic yesterday,' Tobias says, drawing my attention from my phone to the males sitting directly across from me.

'It was a lovely morning meeting everyone. Your pack is very accommodating and welcoming Tobias, and you have some exceptional healers. Kieran and Emma are an asset.'

Tobias seems very satisfied with Diego's response. 'I appreciate you saying that, Diego. We're enjoying having you both here and you're very welcome. Kieran would love some help with a few matters. We have a few pregnant females and a handful of sick pups that he could really use some help with.'

Placing my fork down, I contemplate if I should just leave the table. Tobias knows how I feel about them being here and yet, he doesn't seem to care. He's practically giving them jobs around the place and organising my mating ceremony. He probably wouldn't if he knew the words that we all shared when I did leave Rhiattline. Diego wasn't smooth talking then.

'Thank you, but Luis and I will be leaving in a few days.' His words have everyone stop chatting.

Trying to avoid the numerous eyes staring at me, I end up watching as Luis frowns slightly. The male finishes feeding my beautiful little niece and hands her back to her father.

'I wasn't aware that was the case,' Tobias states, I can feel his eyes boring into my skin. 'We'll be sad to see you go.'

There's a pause that has me deeply uncomfortable so I avert my attention back to my emails.

'So, will you be heading back to Rhiattline? I know you were saying that you had plans to visit a few different packs along the east coast before Diego's role at Claymore begins.'

The simple mention of Claymore has me cringe. That was another reason why we fought. The hospital in Claymore, one of the biggest and most advanced institutions in the country, offered Diego a residency. He's a very gifted doctor.

'We're not sure at the moment. There are a few things we need to work out first,' Luis states and every word is heavy with double meaning.

Again, everyone goes quiet.

'Well, we'll miss having you around,' Sara says sweetly, my sister doesn't seem to be aware of the tension around the table. The baby at on her chest makes a cooing sound.

Tobias and Dom are not being subtle in the way they're frowning at me. Oliver and Liam don't seem too impressed and I'm sure if Ridley, Delfina and Gilly were here, they'd be helping the conversation along.

'I hope I can take up some of your time before you go, Luis. I'd love to learn how to make those meatballs you cooked the other night. Easton and the others loved them,' Adalee enquires, she's so much like my sister. Easton beams at his mate, the goofy look on his face makes my eyes roll.

'Of course. If you're free this afternoon, I'd love to come by and cook with you,' Luis grins towards the female and I can't take it anymore.

The conversations start again. Luis and Diego in the middle of them all, loving every bit of it.

Mama too. She seems very animated this morning. Her attention is fixed on the newcomers and she keeps reaching out and touching Diego's arm while they laugh and talk. He keeps filling her plate with food.

My phone buzzes and I get to work fixing an issue with a partner company, just a little staffing issue.

'I wish you didn't have to go so soon. I've enjoyed having some new faces around the den,' Mama replies to something Luis says.

That's me done.

Rising as calmly as I can, I excuse myself from this lovely breakfast and tell everyone that I have to get ready for work.

Chapter Twenty One

Present Day

'Tobias, I really don't want to have this conversation,' I tell the reflection of my brother in the mirror of my vanity. I've decided on a purple pant-suit and a black blouse for work today. August calls this outfit a 'real power move' and I'm trying to finish up my makeup. Just a little blush and lip. I don't like too much product. It's my hair that requires all my attention. I've already spent the last half an hour getting it to bounce the way I like.

Tobias sits on the chest at the foot of the bed, his focus on the words engraved at the top. 'So, did you work through everything with your mates like I told you to? Not that I need you to tell me the answer seeing as how they're leaving.'

Throwing him a glare, I finish off my face and step back to make sure I'm ready for the day. 'I've asked you not to call them that.'

'And I asked you to deal with this issue, Nic. This isn't dealing with it.'

Spinning on thin heels, I demand to know why this is so important to him. 'Give me a break, Tobias! This is my business. I left Rhiattline and those males behind for a reason. I don't have the luxury like you and Sara to follow my heart, I have work to do.'

Tobias just looks perplexed. 'What? Nicolette, why do you think that?'

I can't do this right now and turn my back on him to head to my jewellery stand near the bed.

Tobias stands and I watch him in my peripherals. My wolf can scent his emotions.

'You know what, Tobias? I can't do this. I have two very important meetings today, one with a new client who could bring in millions of dollars and then I have to be across the city to meet with a start-up company run by two woman who have an awesome idea to create sensory mindful clothing. I loved their presentation and I want to meet them. So, I can't deal with this. I have money to make and multiple companies to run.'

Tobias sits back down and traces that same engraving. 'I remember when Dad worked on this. What did the pack females used to call it?'

He just won't give up. 'A hope box. It's an outdated concept of collecting items to take when you leave pack after you're mated, or to take to your new den to start your new life.'

Nodding as if remembering, Tobias sighs. 'I think everyone was always under the impression that you'd one day leave Farrowline to find your mate. You were always too big for this place, Nicolette. Always been destined to follow your dreams and your spirit.'

Studying myself in the mirror, absorbing Tobias's words, I only see grief. 'Life has a way of changing things, doesn't it.'

'Yeah, it does.' Looking over at my Alpha, I hate the conversation we are having right now. 'How did everything get so mixed up?' Tobias questions softly.

'Because Dad was taken from us. We were robbed of a father and an Alpha, and we had to grow up.'

'Did I make you grow up too fast, Nic? Did I do something wrong by you in those early days?'

It's my turn to sigh and I head over to sit down beside my big, annoying and fiercely loyal brother. His body takes up most of the chest but I manage as best I can.

'You didn't make me do anything, Tobias. What happened threw the entire pack off its axis. We all had to step up. You, Dom, Oliver, Liam, Easton, and me. We were the next generation. The moment Dad passed was the moment we all had to grow up and take our place in pack.'

Tobias sets those familiar eyes on me. They are sad and I see the weight my brother has had to hold since the moment that gun went off. This is why I do what I do. It's not just Mama and Sara, or the Pack, it's because of him too. My big, absurdly protective brother who had the biggest responsibility thrown upon him when he was too young.

'But should I've done things differently?'

This is a side of Tobias that not everyone sees. The male behind the Alpha. I'm glad he has Ridley and Noah now. My brother changed when he found his mate. There was a few years there where we were getting worried about him. He was too hard. Too quick to anger. Now, he reminds me of dad. Grounded and calmer.

It's amazing what one little human can do. Two humans, if you include Noah.

'We did the best we could, Tobias. We all did.' And that's the truth.

Chapter Twenty Two

NICOLETTE IS NINETEEN

Running through the rain, I let my wolf take control over my body without shifting. I run and run and wish that I could leave everything behind. It has been a month and the pain is getting worse. Nothing is getting easier despite how many times everyone tells me that time will heal this pain.

Nothing can heal the cracks that've formed in my family and my heart. Mama is still not getting out of bed. Sara is barely eating and Tobias is so busy around Pack that I haven't spoken to him in three days.

Dom, Oliver, Liam and Easton haven't left my brothers side, which I'm grateful for, but I wished they'd see that I need help too. That I'm trying desperately to not let Mama go. To get Sara to continue her studies and eat.

Shouting to the cloudy sky, I wish for answers. Sitting around pack is killing me.

Legs pumping, I run until I hit the edge of the farthest corner of territory and swing back around to follow the imaginary line. I don't stop. I let the rain soak me through. Relish in the way my muscles scream and free my tears.

Lost in my mind, I almost miss the way my wolf picks up on the lone figure sitting in the rain under a tree.

Coming to an abrupt halt, I bend over and grip my knees, my chest heaving as I stare at the male crying thick, violent tears in the darkness.

My already broken heart splinters and cracks even further.

Stifling a whimper of my own at the sight, I make my way slowly to where Tobias is curled up, feeling his grief.

I know he is aware of me and I fall beside him on the muddy ground and throw my arms around his giant body.

Head resting on his back, I cry along with him and offer my presence as support.

'I'm trying, Nic. This is too much.' His words break me.

'I know, Tobias. You're doing an exceptional job. The Pack is healing and it's all because of you.'

'There are too many things to juggle and I feel like I'm failing. Now, more than ever, we need to be strong, and yet, I can't be here and at Farrow Group. I'm afraid that if I let the business fall, we will suffer. I know no one sees the true value in this company, but Nic, we can make it successful. We can make the Pack money so that no one has to worry.'

Tobias has always been so passionate about Farrow Group. Dominic and Liam are just as invested in making this work and I've never really been around enough to pay much attention. I was never going to be here.

I was supposed to start my studies in Blighton and I should be living in Rhiattline right now.

I don't ask if Liam and Dom can pick up the slack. The pair are just as busy. We have a completely new Circle and positions have to change. Some elders have stepped down from active roles and grieving mates are still a massive worry as we try to bring in a new generation for Farrowline.

'I have so many plans and yet, I can't find the time to even grieve that Dad is gone. I don't know what to do.' It's not his sadness that has me make my next decision. It's the complete and utter lack of emotion. I just hug him tighter.

'Tell me what to do? How can I help?' I ask his back, refusing to let him go.

'You're already doing too much. I should be looking after—'

'Tobias, please,' I cut him off, I don't need any more sympathy. I'm sick of everyone trying to check in on me or sneaking food into my fridge. I know that I screwed up by leaving Dad alone. I know it was all my fault. I should've stayed and fought. I should have died next to my alpha. Tobias would've. It doesn't matter that he told me to go. I should've ignored his command. 'Let me help. I need to help or I think I'll go crazy.'

'Thanks Nic, but you don't know how to run a business. You're only nineteen.'

'I'm a quick learner, brother. Leave it with me. You only have four employees for fuck's sake. I've been helping the family run a pack since I was ten, I think I can manage.'

'Nic—'

'Tobias, I need to do this,' I implore, having something to do, a job like this might help. It has too. 'Let me help.'

That night, after I feed Sara and Mama, I set up my laptop and get to work understanding what I need to know in order to make up for everything I have done to break my pack.

Nothing can bring back my dad, and I'm not an alpha, but I can make this Pack successful and ensure that no one will want for anything. That is what I can do for failing my family.

I will help build Farrow Group and create the richest pack in the country.

I'm a Farrow. This is my pack too.

Chapter Twenty Three

Present Day

'Don't start!' I warn August just as he sits in the seat across from me. It's getting late and he has only just ushered a group of women out of the office who came to show me a rack full of ballgowns. The entire appointment lasted twenty minutes and I now have two dresses, plus accessories, and a very grumpy assistant. Mostly because I didn't listen to August's advice once.

'I didn't say anything.'

'You didn't need to, your face is saying enough.'

'Well, if you want to look like an elder at the gala events, then go right ahead.'

Sighing, I give up trying to write this email. August is looking at his own device with a dramatic scowl on his face. 'I don't look like an elder. It was two, ten thousand dollar gowns, one with lace sleeves, and the other with a high neckline, what's wrong with sleeves and a neckline?'

'Nothing, if you're eighty years old.'

Growling low, I refuse to talk about this anymore. The dresses I chose were elegant and gorgeous and didn't show half my arse or my breasts like the ones August wanted me to try on.

'Let's move on shall we?' Augusts purrs like a real smartass.

'So, tell me what happened with Patrick Gravelly, Ridley wasn't happy about something, but I missed half of what was said as I dealt—'

I'm cut off when one of the interns I have working the front desk today pokes her head through the door.

'Sorry, Ms Farrow,' the poor young human looks like she is about to have a stroke addressing me.

'What's wrong? You can't just open the door like that,' August states a little too ruffly.

'August,' I warn. 'What is it?' I ask, trying to keep my annoyance out of my tone.

'Sorry to disturb, but a Mr Cortez is here and he, um, he said that he's your mate, Ms Farrow, so he doesn't need an appointment.'

Her eyes are wide and I realise my wolf has made a noise that has scared her.

August is on his feet before I can get over my shock of hearing that Luis is here. 'Let him in, don't leave Ms Farrow's mate waiting.' He seems way too excited about Luis being here.

'August!' I reprimand, for what in particular, I don't know. Now the entire office is going to be gossiping all afternoon and won't get any work done.

The bear shifter just waves off my annoyance and shoos the intern away and pulls open the door fully, and sure enough there is Luis standing just outside the door looking like sex on legs.

His hair is all messy and falls around his face. That youthful smile on his full lips and that jawline, has my panties instantly wet. Thighs clench together at the sight, I don't miss that half the office is standing, watching the show. For heaven's sake!

'Mr Cortez,' August says in his most professional tone. I could smack him.

'Sorry for interrupting,' Luis replies in that smooth, deep voice. His grey eyes drift to me before they move to my assistant. He holds out his hand in greeting. 'You must be the famous August.'

August appears to be having some kind of episode as he takes it and starts blabbering about how amazing it is to finally meet him. Luis doesn't seem at all bothered by the bear shifter's excitement and converses easily with him, giving my assistant his full attention. That's what Luis does, he makes you feel like you are the only one in the world. Or at least that is how he made me feel.

'Please come in and sit. I'll leave you two alone.' August completely ignores my glare and is practically skipping around ushering Luis in. He heads towards the door. 'Ms Farrow,' he says before he shuts it fully. Arsehole has a twinkle in his eyes as he smiles at me. 'I'll hold all your calls.'

I send a quick text to him informing my, *now ex-assistant,* that I'm firing him tomorrow, before placing my phone down on the desk. I sit for a few minutes just watching Luis walk around my office. It's weird seeing him in my space. I honestly thought that he didn't want anything to do with me after the way we left it back in Rhiattline. He broke my heart when I didn't think I had a heart for him to break.

The silence isn't awkward as he runs his hands over every surface. 'I came to say that if you're avoiding your den because Diego and I are there then we will leave, Nicolette. It's not what we want.'

His words take a moment to sink it and I don't know what makes my heartrate spike more, the fact that he said he will leave or that he called me Nicolette. Luis never says my name.

'I'm working, Luis. This is what I do.'

Luis stops in front of an oil painting above the side table across the room. His head moves from side to side slowly as he assesses the piece that cost way too much money. 'This isn't very good,' he says to the blue and white mess of a picture. 'I'm surprised you picked it.

'I didn't,' I reply. 'One of the staff organised the décor. It's not really my job.'

Luis throws me an odd look over his shoulder, 'and what is your job?'

I don't know why that question rubs me the wrong way. 'I run multiple companies, Luis. I advise and fund hundreds more. I sit on five committees and charity boards. I am the Chief Operating Officer here at Farrow Group. The list goes on and on,' I state, unsure why I'm grumpy. Maybe it's because everyone has been discussing my work recently and the amount of time I spend making the money that supports Farrowline.

'That is a lot of jobs. And what do you do, for you? Where is your art in this world, bonita? Where is the Nicolette that I met in Rhiattline, the one I fell in love with? Because she isn't in this place.'

This is twice now he has made that comment.

I'm so lost in my own head that I miss what he says next and he has to repeat himself a few times when he asks me to go to lunch with him. 'Show me the city so that I might understand better the decisions that you've made.'

I only agree because I'm hungry and he throws me those puppy eyes that always make me swoon.

'Fine, we'll go down to the café down the street,' I declare, rising from behind my desk. The stupid triumphant look on his face has me rethink everything I've just said. 'You're paying!'

I head to the door of my office without making sure that he is following and curse my stupid wolf when she shivers at the sensual chuckle that comes from behind me.

Growling in frustration, I yank open the door and gape down at the male who swears colourfully and falls on the floor before me.

'What are you doing?' I snap and watch as August jumps to his feet with a wide grin, he doesn't even defend the fact that he was eavesdropping. Hands on hips, I growl again. 'Are you not busy enough, August? I can find some other work for you to do!'

'No need Ms Farrow,' the fool grins and I huff and walk past him. I know Luis is close behind. 'I should work on my resume as I'll be needing it tomorrow to apply for a new job.'

Smart-arse.

Chapter Twenty Four

PRESENT DAY

'I LIKE AUGUST,' LUIS declares, stepping up beside me the moment we leave the building and head out on to the streets of South Sylo.

'Of course you do,' I grumble and navigate the busyness of the city. There are shifters and humans everywhere.

Luis asks a few questions and exclaims his love of the city while I try to not engage with his infectious excitement. This is why I've made a point of keeping my distance from this male. Luis consumes my world when I'm around him and I have a way of losing my head in his presence.

'Are you not going to talk to me?' Luis asks.

We're both navigating the sidewalk as best we can. Me, walking as fast as possible, and Luis trying to keep up while he takes in the spectacular view of South Sylo. The buildings here are tall and covered in greenery and hanging gardens. Nature and the human made elements working in harmony to create balance. 'I see the appeal of this place.'

'Yes, the city is nice,' I reply absently and step around a mother with a stroller and then side-eying Luis when he navigates the space so that he is directly to my right again. Frustration growing at what I think he is doing, I make a point of moving around to stand on his other side and then growl when he makes a point of appearing at my right again as if keeping his position between me and the busy road. Protecting me from the traffic.

'Stop that!' I snap and try and fail to be the one standing between the traffic and the male. He refuses to give up his position and all I get is a smirk in response. Absurd dominant males and their need to always be the protector in a group. It grinds my gears and rubs me the wrong way.

'Luis!' I warn when he continues to 'protect' me.

'Humour me, love,' is all I get, and so I do, only because arguing with him on the streets of South Sylo isn't something I have the energy for this afternoon.

We get to the café and find our seats without another word. Once we've ordered and received our food, I try to come up with something to say and fall short. Luis has the attention of many people in the place and yet, his eyes have never drifted off me.

'I'm making you nervous.'

'No,' I reply too quickly. 'It's weird having you in my world.'

'I can imagine. My intention is not to make you uncomfortable. I just want to get to know who you are here. I feel like I barely know you. How everyone speaks of you in Farrowline makes me unsure what is real.'

I stop playing with my food and stare at him, just to see if I can understand his tone. 'What do they say about me in Farrowline?'

Luis throws me one of his signature smiles. 'Nothing bad. Everyone loves and respects you. You work hard for your pack and they all know that. However, they speak about Nicolette the business female. The straight-talking, dominant who is barely off her device and always busy. Not the shifter I met in Rhiattline all those months ago. The one who painted Diego and I in the ocean with such passion that I nearly wept. You're different here and I hope to find out why.'

'I need to get back to work,' I say, not sure how to feel or what to say. I am different here. He isn't wrong. 'Are you okay to get back to Farrowline?'

'Yes, amor, I'll be fine. I may explore the city for a bit. Maybe visit the Art Gallery,' Luis states, his grey eyes are sad which makes me sad. 'I will see you back at the den.'

Nodding, I leave knowing that every step I take makes me deeply uncomfortable.

Chapter Twenty Five

Nicolette in Rhiattline

I wake feeling like I've had a near-death experience and nearly drowned.

Oh yeah...right.

I guess I deserve the pain assaulting every muscle in my body. The groan that comes from my lips is a mix between animal and human. I've opened my eyes to the world spinning, again.

Vision blurry, I'm assaulted with the scents of summer. One of the sun on the sand and the other of the heat on salty water. Closing my eyes is the only option I have. Even though my nose keeps my mind from slipping into darkness. The aroma in the bungalow is intoxicating. I want to ask what's on the menu but all I can muster is a weak mumble for some water. A strong hand gently cups the back of my head and helps me to rise.

'Small sips, amor,' the deep voice says, leaving no room to disobey. *Amor.* I have heard that a great deal since being stuck in this bed. I want to ask them what that means but the words don't come easily. Everything is so fuzzy. I manage to only spill a little of the water which is better than what I did last time I managed to claw my way out of the darkness. Not that I can't feel it still, the darkness is there in my mind, ready to suck me back into oblivion.

Time has no meaning. I have no idea how long I've been in this bed. I have lost count of the many times I've woken and have been spoon-fed and looked after. Every time I tell myself to protest, I find the words slip from my mind to be left with compliance. My wolf is content and secure to let us be taken care of.

I'm just so unbelievably tired.

The bed dips to the side and as I'm unable to turn my head, another large hand comes to lift me up so that I can drink down the savoury broth from the spoon placed against my lips. It's the perfect temperature. Warm and comforting. The taste of it explodes in my mouth and my next groan is from joy at eating something so divine.

'That's it, just a bit more,' Luis soothes and continues to feed me.

Diego is at my arm while I eat, taking my blood pressure and softly telling me what he's doing while Luis encourages me to keep eating.

'I'm going to give you some pain killers, Nicolette. It'll get rid of the pain in your head and you can sleep a little more easily. This infection hasn't broken yet.'

I grunt in acknowledgement. My head hurts so much that my eyes feel like they are being squeezed. I know that I'm really unwell and been battling a fever for a while now. I'm grateful that it is dark in the bungalow and after being told to be ready for the small scratch that never feels like a scratch, the painkiller Diego just administered works almost immediately.

'I hope you have a proper degree in medicine,' I mumble and hear the male still sitting on bed laugh softly.

'Our Diego is very qualified,' Luis reassures me. His hand moves from the back of my neck to run his fingers down my face in an attempt to speak to my wolf and reassure her of her safety. It's unnecessary but appreciated by the beast under my skin.

'Too bad if I wasn't,' is the 'healer's' curt reply. 'I'm sure my head would be separated from my body if I treated the sister of the Alpha of Farrowline with anything but the best possible care. Or so we've been told.'

That has my eyes opening a little. 'Told?' I whisper because the spinning room is making my stomach churn and I'm afraid I'm going to vomit everywhere.

'Yes, your phone doesn't stop ringing and we had a very interesting chat with your brother earlier,' Diego doesn't sound too impressed. Frankly, he sounds a little annoyed and I can only imagine what was said. Tobias is an alpha for a reason and while I don't question the dominance of these two, I know what it's like being told to do something by the Alpha of Farrowline.

'Please tell me you didn't tell him what happened.' Damn. That's the last thing I need. I try to get up and am stopped by Luis.

His large hand falls to my shoulder. 'We didn't tell him anything, just that you were unwell and being looked after,' he reassures me and then says a few hurried and harsh sounding words to Diego that I can't interpret. It sounds like he's reprimanding the male but I don't know them well enough to know their dynamic.

I don't have the energy to keep my eyes open any longer and I drift off to sleep, pain-free.

The next time I'm able to open my eyes it's to a strong, calloused hand against my forehead. It feels amazing. I whimper. My mouth is full of saliva and I feel my stomach protesting even though there is nothing in it.

I move just as I begin to heave and feel the body on the bed beside me. He helps me to roll, while the other male tilts my head and brings me gently to the side of the mattress to throw up in a waiting pan. The only thing keeping me from completely losing it is the two voices that sooth my mind, telling me that I am safe and secure. That I'm not alone.

Chapter Twenty Six

Nicolette in Rhiattline

Sitting up in bed, I stare out the window, completely stunned at how heavy the rain outside is falling. I woke to the sound of the storm and rub at my pounding head. It feels like it's about to split in two. My mouth is dry. My mind is all hazy still and I hate that it doesn't seem like I'm getting any better.

'You're awake. How's the headache?' A deep male voice questions to my right. Diego is fiddling with the bag of supplies he keeps next to the bed.

'Where is my phone?' I ask instead. I don't think I've slept this much in my life and I finally feel a little less...disorientated.

'Over there,' Diego states with a small head gesture to the table on my other side. He clearly has some kind of issue with it. Still, I grab it and read through the first ten emails before my eyes go all blurry and I have to place it back down.

'Looking at a screen for a prolonged period of time will exacerbate your symptoms.' I have an overwhelming need to roll my eyes at the very doctor explanation of why he has been keeping the device away from me. 'It doesn't stop buzzing. How do you stand it?'

I don't know what it is about this male but he makes me feel like an adolescent again, my insides feel as if they're full of butterflies but I won't delve into that. Not when he's so close I can smell him. Diego is the sun on the ocean, like salt and crashing waves. Full of energy and danger. 'You're a very busy female, it seems.'

'Yes, I am, and lying around in your bungalow is not using my time wisely.' Taking the small pills Diego hands me, I down them quickly with the water he passes over. I've been in this bed for days, I know the drill. I wake up. He hands me pills, or if I'm too sick, he gives me a shot. Luis feeds me as much as I can stomach and then I pass out. Today I feel a little different though. Sore but my eyes don't feel as heavy and there isn't a crease between Diego's brow like I've become accustomed to.

'You need to recover,' Diego states like I'm silly to think that it's a waste of time to be doing nothing. 'You'll need to be in bed for a few more days. You hit your head harder than we originally thought. You ingested sea water and the cut on your head became infected. You need to rest, I suggest you stay in bed for the next seven days.'

'I don't think any of my clients or employees care that I'm neglecting them so that I can recover from a knock on the head. Seven days is not going to happen.' I don't mean for my words to be so harsh but that's how it comes out.

Needing to use the bathroom and dying for a shower, I sit up with a groan and throw my legs over the side of the bed. I hate feeling this weak. I was an idiot to go into that ocean.

I need to take a moment to get over the spinning before I can try and move again.

'You need to lie back down, Nicolette.'

'I need to use the bathroom, and I want to take a shower.'

Diego makes a noise behind me that I don't acknowledge. He can huff all he likes, I need to get up before my wolf takes over and rips him to shreds.

I don't have the luxury to take days to recover. The last three were the longest I've ever stopped working and I got pneumonia when I was twenty two.

'Do you need help?' Diego asks and I swear if I could muster up the energy, I'd use my claws on him. I must be hearing things because he chuckles. I didn't think he'd have a sense of humour.

Luis appears before me and crouches down so that I can see his handsome face. His black rimmed glasses add to the gorgeous features. They accentuate his high cheekbones and I have a silly need to reach out and touch his face. 'We could always give you a sponge bath, bonita. Diego and I will be very gentle.'

It takes me a moment to understand what he's just said and when I do, I fucking giggle. Snapping my mouth shut, I can't help but frown deeply. I don't remember the last time I giggled. Luis's grey eyes are bright and full of victory. Damn male wolf and damn my own who opens her eyes and stretches under my skin, all of a sudden feeling much better and curious as to how they would both taste. 'No, thank you. I'll pass.'

His hands come up to rest on my knees. 'The offer is always there.' I nearly swallow my tongue at the velvety tone and end up staring into his captivating eyes like I'm stuck.

'Luis,' Diego says in a tone I'm very familiar with. It's all dominant male. The next few words the pair speaks are beautiful and full of life, if only I was able to understand what they're saying. Luis throws me a cheeky smile before he gets up and tells me that he'll get the shower ready.

He leaves and I have an overwhelming need to ask him to come back and help me get to the bathroom. My ego stops me. Instead, I just sit, unable to find the strength to rise.

Staring at the hand that appears under my nose, I have to really put away my pride. There's no way I can get to the other side of the bungalow on my own.

Luis is whistling around the space. I have no idea what he's doing and get a glimpse of him walking around with a small pile of towels and product before he flicks on the bathroom light. The sight of the tiled room has me focus on how badly I need to use the facilities. Damn it!

I reach out and place my hand within the healers outstretched one and feel the calluses against my skin as it closes around my fingers. The heat of his touch is nothing like I've ever experienced and for a moment all I can do is stare at our joined hands. His is so much bigger than mine, which isn't necessarily what has me pause. It's the strength of his hold. The way it makes me feel.

Safe.

'Nicolette?' Gaze slowly rising to Diego's, I stare into the strangest lavender depths I've ever seen. 'Let me help you get where you need to go.'

His words take me off guard. There is so much meaning in them and so many reasons why every hair on my body stands on end.

Chapter Twenty Seven

Nicolette in Rhiattline

With Diego way too close and my ego well and truly stomped all over, I have to lean on him to be able to get to the other side of the bungalow. What makes the entire situation worse is that my wolf is rolling around under my skin, basking in his scent. Every step is torture with the heat that pools between my legs. She wants to take over and this time it's to devour the poor male beside me.

Diego doesn't say a thing despite the fact that he would definitely scent my growing desire. The rain on the roof and the thunder that shakes the foundation adds to the cloud of lust growing in my mind.

When I step into the bathroom, the light flickers with the next round of thunder and I push away from the healer to grab at the sink. Everything is white and grey. The shower is bigger than the one in the pink cabin and I look at it longingly.

I have been lying in bed for days and I smell like it. I smell my stupidity and I wish to wash it off and forget my near death experience.

Luis turns on the shower and really this space isn't big enough for the three of us. Their combined scents are choking and intoxicating and utterly confusing.

Again, the storm outside has the windows rattle. I forgot how intense the weather is out here in Rhiattline.

Diego stands at the door, watching me closely while Luis stays near the shower, checking the water temperature like I'm some kind of pup who might scald herself. When he's finished, I end up standing at the counter, using it to hold me up and stare at the two males who are making no move to leave. I notice my bag of toiletries and my small carry bag of clothes that one of them must have gotten from the pink bungalow. I don't know how it makes me feel seeing my stuff here or that they took the privilege of touching my belongings without asking. It's a little forward and does nothing to help me calm my wolf. She loves it. She wants them to touch more than just my belongings.

'I can take it from here, thank you both,' I manage to say through a very dry throat and it has nothing to do with being thirsty for water. No, my wolf is thirsty for something completely different.

'Are you sure, bonita? I can help and I won't look at anything. I promise,' Luis replies too formally. I hear the hint of amusement and arousal.

Glaring at the male through the mirror, who is still testing the water, I shake my head and instantly regret it when a wave of dizziness and nausea sweeps over me.

I swear I hear Diego mumble that I'm a stubborn female but ignore it. They haven't seen the half of it and they've clearly never met a Farrow before. Stubborn is our middle name.

Besides, I don't know if I can control my wolf for much longer and if Luis or Diego help me get naked, I genuinely have no idea how it will end.

I don't even know them. It must be because they saved my life that I now feel some kind of connection.

The pair share a look and it's pretty clear that they know how badly I'm struggling to hold myself together.

When Luis brushes up against me as he passes, telling me that he is just outside if I need anything, I have to bite the inside of my lip to keep from asking him to stay. To help me quench this unbearable heat.

What the hell is wrong with me?

When the door is closed, I give myself the best talking to of my life. I channel my inner Ridley with the foul words I use to tell myself to get my shit together. I have no idea what this heat is but it needs to stop. Right. Now.

Reprimanding myself silently in the mirror, I study how my honey coloured eyes are way too hooded and how my thick, black curls are all tangled and knotted around my face, like a rats nest. I have an overwhelming desire to smack myself in the face. This is not who I am. I don't fawn over males. I don't go into a weird kind of heat because of their scent and I don't lose my head over how attractive they are. And damn they are attractive.

Both of them are as equally compelling. A complete contrast. One is mischievous and gorgeous. The other harder and mouthwatering. I want to get to know them both. I want to ask them questions and understand what kind of connection they have with each other because it feels as if they are a two-shifter pack and that is confusing. The energy that surrounds them is perfectly balanced and has thrown mine off-centre. The way they interact is fascinating. The glances and the perfect harmony hint to a life and bond forged from something more than just a friendship or love. They don't smell like lovers. They smell like two bound individuals within the same pack. It is utterly confusing.

I honestly have no idea how I manage to use the facilities and stumble into the shower without injuring myself too badly. I have a giant bruise forming on my shin from smacking into the cabinet, but I'll live.

Head resting against the cool tiles as the water flows down my back, I try to focus my mind away from my situation and to what matters. I need to contact Farrowline and make sure that everything is okay in the office. I should ring Mama and Sara. What I won't be telling anyone is that I nearly died in the ocean. I can remember that Diego and Luis told me they spoke to Tobias and I have to trust that they didn't tell him anything about what happened. They can't know. I'm supposed to be the even-headed one. The one to look after everyone, not the fool who goes for a swim fully clothed in the middle of the off-season.

Stepping from the shower and towelling off is just as difficult as I thought it would be and I end up needing to sit on the edge of the oval shaped bath. With the towel wrapped around me, I shiver and battle with the overwhelming need to lash out and break something. I'm not weak. I'm an independent female who can look after herself and have been doing so since I was nineteen years old and yet, the distance between me and my bag of clothes feels impossible. My stupid lip wobbles.

What is wrong with me?

Chapter Twenty Eight

Nicolette in Rhiattline

'Bonita?' A soft knock on the door has me gain control over my emotions. Luis's voice is full of warmth as he says, 'beautiful, let us in to help you. We can scent your exhaustion. I promise we will not look or touch you in any way that you do not consent to.'

I want to shout back that half of what he has said is the problem, I truly don't know what my wolf will consent to right now. Instead, I don't respond right away. It may have something to do with the way my heart pounds in my chest.

'Nicolette,' the next voice states. The tone isn't sweet like Luis. No, Diego speaks like he expects everyone in the room to listen. His knock isn't even nice, it's brisk and to the point, and fuck me, it turns me on. 'I am a healer. There's nothing that you have that I haven't seen before.'

Not that he can see it but I glare at the door. He did probably hear the small growl I just made. I don't care. He just continues like I'm being unreasonable.

'I think it best you allow us to come in and assist you. You'll make yourself sicker and then you will need to stay here with us longer.'

'Come now, beautiful,' Luis casual voice filters through the closed door, 'you don't want that, do you?' I can hear the smile in his tone. He's teasing me.

'No,' I reply and then wish I could take the words back. I spoke without thinking and I never do that. They take that as an invitation and I guess it was.

Soon the bathroom is too small with the two dominant males in the space.

I clutch the towel tighter and watch silently as Luis moves to the bag and places it down gently at my foot. He crouches down to it. There aren't many clothes within, a few comfortable items. I don't say a word as he pulls out a pair of grey trackpants and neither does he as he slowly lifts his eyes to mine. The seriousness has me forget about the dizziness and the way my head is spinning. Every muscle in my body tenses as his large, masculine hands gently run down the side of my legs. With a tenderness that threatens to shatter every wall I have constructed around my heart, he begins to help me dress.

I rub at the space between my breasts to try and rid myself of the ache that begins there.

Painfully slow, Luis helps me to step into the pants. Diego moves to my right and then the lights flicker when the next wave of thunder hits the world. We all pause when the room is plunged into darkness.

Not one word is spoken as we stand in the dark. The only light coming through the small window behind me is the flashes of lightning. My eyes adjust to the lack of light thanks to the nocturnal hunter in my blood.

The males surrounding me continue their task and as Luis' hands travel up my legs as he helps me into my pants, I bite back a moan. I don't have to be a tracker to pick up on the growing lust. I'm no longer sure if I'm lightheaded because of the concussion or because of my desire.

Diego grips my arm and gently helps me to my feet, his hold unwavering and sure as he assists me to stand as Luis dresses me. Their combined hands on my skin has my heart flutter. I can feel their gazes as if they have a weight. Their heat calms my rolling stomach and I close my eyes and lean into Diego's warmth in a moment that I know will have a profound impact on my life. I haven't had such care and devotion showered upon me in what feels like forever. No one looks after me. I don't allow myself to be vulnerable. I lost that privilege when I ran from my responsibilities and my duty at nineteen and left my father to die on his own.

Diego's hand travels along the arm I have gripping the towel to cover my chest and I have no idea if it is his doing or if I let go, but the towel slips away, leaving my chest fully bare.

Right now, in this moment, it doesn't matter that I have no idea who they are. That I have only just met them. My wolf and I are completely at ease.

I am a female who pursues her desires. I don't feel any kind of embarrassment. My nipples harden. Diego and Luis make a deep sound in the back of their throat that has me sway on my feet.

However, I haven't given any kind of consent for them to touch me, so they don't. When Luis bends and rises with one of my shirts in his hand, I lift my arms as best I can with my head pounding and shiver when the fabric caresses my skin.

Luis steps so close, I could kiss him, and when the shirt goes over my head and I come face to face with the gorgeous male, I think that is exactly what he is going to do.

Without me giving permission, the male smirks as if he knows how hard I'm trying to keep myself together. He bends and grabs my jumper and helps me wiggle into it. All the while Diego watches, keeping me steady.

It's the most intense moment of my life.

And the most confusing.

Chapter Twenty Nine

Nicolette in Rhiattline

Aunt El visits me the next morning and even with Diego barking orders that I shouldn't be out of bed, I curl up on the comfy outdoor chair on the small patio of the bungalow cradling a tea.

Aunt El keeps throwing me these little looks and smirking that I'm trying desperately to ignore. My head is still hurting and the pain is radiating down my neck and into my shoulders. Diego wasn't very pleased when I told him what I was feeling earlier and insisted that I was only *allowed* to go as far as the patio to meet with my aunt.

'So, I spoke to your mum and your brother this morning.'

Mug hovering just shy of my lips, I look quickly over at my aunt and regret the sudden movement instantly. 'What? Why? What did you say?' I haven't spoken to anyone in Farrowline yet. I know Diego and Luis have but I can't seem to find the energy to have an argument with Tobias or Mum about what happened.

Aunt El smiles, her light blue eyes all full of mischief. I swear she is so much like Mama, well at least mum back when dad was still alive.

There is a sadness to my mum's eyes that never goes away now. Aunt El doesn't have that. She is full of laughter and hasn't changed much over the years.

'That you hurt your head and that you're being looked after by two guests of Rhiattline. Tobias nearly sent the very handsome Jaxon to come and get you. I have to say I was pretty disappointed when your Luna got involved and told the males of Farrowline to calm down and wait until you actually ring to let them know you would like their help.'

Thank the heavens for Ridley, she's the only one they listen to and the only one who seems to think before acting. I have to place down my tea on the little table beside the chair to keep from laughing when El says the exact thing I'm thinking. She's right when she says that having a Farrowline male come here stomping around knowing I'm hurt is the last thing I need right now.

'You never actually said how you did it though. Diego and Luis have been pretty vague with the story when they were asked,' Aunt El enquires leaning forward and studying my face like she's making sure that I'm not going to fall off the chair and die suddenly.

Clearing my throat, I pull the blanket Luis insisted I drape over my legs further up my body. 'I fell down the stairs at the pink bungalow. Silly accident. I'm lucky that Luis and Diego were close.'

One eyebrow raised, El makes a noise that tells me she isn't convinced. 'Right.' I guess I can't blame her, I'm not known for being clumsy. Actually, admitting that I fell down some stairs is very uncharacteristic of me. I don't fall over. 'I trust that you are being well looked after.' Looking around, El leans forward again and says, 'they're very handsome, aren't they?'

'I guess,' I reply, making sure that the two males who I've had a hard time looking at today after our intense bathroom moment last night aren't close. I'm lying and El knows it because she grins wide.

'I can't express how much of a stir they kicked up when they arrived. You have to meet their sister, she is a beautiful soul. We are all so honoured to have her in our pack. Her mating ceremony is what brings everyone here.' That's news to me, I didn't realise.

'Their sister?' I ask, hungry for more information. I vaguely remember that Luis may have mentioned something about that. Even after the intense short time I have known them, I don't have any real idea of who they are. I didn't realise that they are brothers. They don't smell like blood relatives, packmates, yes, but not blood.

'Well, she is Diego's sister but once you get to know these two males, you will realise that they are brothers in all ways but blood. They followed Gloria when she received a scholarship at the university. The trio are a pack unto themselves. Bound in ways I'm afraid none of us truly know. There has definitely been pain shared and packmates lost along the way. Luis is the only one who speaks of the harshness of the country they came from.'

Processing what she's telling me, I find myself deeply interested and moved by her words. The idea that Luis and Diego have come from such a traumatic and difficult past makes me really upset. I've only just met them but in that moment, I know that there is more to this. That the way my wolf growls in my head emphasises that her and I are growing an attachment unlike any other that she has felt before.

'The Alpha was overjoyed to hear that Diego was a healer, he is exceptional. There is talk that he is waiting to see if he gets some big temporary position at a hospital across the country. No one wants to bring it up. We are hoping that they'll stay here and make Rhiattline their permanent pack.' She takes a breath and just when I think she has finished, El says, 'And have you heard Luis play his guitar and sing yet?' She clutches her chest dramatically. 'It's like something from the heavens. He could make packs go to war or declare peace with that voice. I've seen many a female and male offer to warm his bed after a performance.'

'You know they can probably hear you,' I remind the female who should be acting a great deal older than what she is right now. I love her energy though. I see so much of Mama in Aunt El and I see so much that we have lost since the death of my father.

'Oh honey, I know they can.' She winks and I can't help but laugh out loud, my head rewarding me by pounding harder. 'So, do you think you'll be better by tomorrow? Some of the females are going into town for lunch and shopping. Or should I ask your carers?'

'Stop it,' I warn, fighting with the way my mouth pulls at the edges. Grabbing my tea again, I process everything that El has just said as she continues chatting about the upcoming mating ceremony and how the Alpha of Rhiattline would like me to come to dinner when I am well. He apparently came around early this morning when I was asleep and Diego told him that I wasn't to be disturbed.

I don't know how I feel about that. I don't know how I feel about any of this to be honest. What I *do* know is that I need to grab my things and move to the pink bungalow. Today. I need to put some distance between myself and the males who have gotten under my skin.

I pack up the small bag Luis brought over from the pink bungalow.

'I said seven days in bed,' Diego states for the third time. He is sitting at the small round table doing something on his tablet that requires his full attention.

'And I said that I'm feeling fine and will get out of your way.'

'Can I persuade you to stay for dinner at least?' Luis asks and I have no idea why he sounds like he is laughing at me. While it does smell amazing and my stomach hasn't stopped rumbling since I came inside after saying goodbye to Aunt El, I refuse as politely as I can. 'Come now, bonita. You have to eat. I'll pack you some if you don't want to stay.'

'No, I think—'

'Save your breath, Nicolette, he'll do it anyway,' Diego says casually as he flicks through whatever he is reading on his tablet. Luis hums a gorgeous tune as he moves around the kitchenette. It smells like saffron and rice and chicken and garlic. I want to bottle the smell and wear it as a perfume.

I make quick work of packing everything but when I get to the door and turn around to thank them, I don't really know what I'm saying thank you for. For saving me. For taking care of me. So I end up just telling them that I appreciate what they've done and leave.

Later that afternoon, I'm sitting at the at the end of the cold bed looking at the lifeless cabin. I refuse to admit that I'm feeling the absence of the two males when I smell something familiar.

Opening the front door, I frown down at the package of food containers and then over at the blue building to my right. The lights are on and the music playing from within is like a beacon calling to me.

With a heavy sigh, I bend down and grab the offered food.

Chapter Thirty

Nicolette in Rhiattline

Blighton. I never thought I'd be back here. This town had such a special place in my heart for such a long time. It feels like a different lifetime. I was so young when I was here last. I was an adolescent, walking the streets with Mum and Dad while we looked at the art school I eventually applied for. It was one of many universities that they both came with me to visit.

I loved that Dad was with me. That weekend is one of my favourite memories. It didn't matter how busy Dad was with pack business, he always made sure that I knew that I was his priority. He did the same for Sara and Tobias. We were always his focus.

The group I'm here with headed towards the shopping mall the moment we got to town, I decided to go toward the large park in its centre and the massive art school building that still takes my breath away. It's exactly as I remember it. Stone walls. Archways. Gardens, and all these buildings, including an art gallery where art from around the world is showcased.

Turning my phone to silent, I enter the more modern building and greet the lady behind the counter who welcomes me to the art gallery. I take the map she hands me and start my own self-guided tour of a place I dreamed would one day house one of my pieces.

It was a big dream.

I was young and naive.

I walk the halls of the gallery, stopping and admiring paintings and sculptures for what feels like hours. I carve out time for myself and completely ignore the buzzing device in the back pocket of my loose fitting, high waisted red pants.

Standing before an oil painting created hundreds of years ago, I take in the magnitude of it. It spans the entire wall and depicts a moment in time where a female alpha sacrificed everything for her pack. The title is simply *The Alpha* and it makes me want to weep. I remember standing in this exact position when I was younger and I asked my dad what it meant. His words still ring in my ears.

'It is a depiction of everything it means to be an alpha, Letti.'

I could never understand why anyone would want to be a leader if this is how life was for them, and I told him that. My dad just laughed and pointed out the many faces in the painting. I look at them now. The wolves. The humans. *'Look at them, daughter. This is why she does it. For them. You can see the love in their expressions. The pure devotion. She is their heart, Letti. She is made for them. She goes to her next life knowing that packmates who have already gone before her are there waiting, and the ones that will follow after, will find her eventually.'*

'That's sad.'

'It is sweetheart. But, it's also beautiful and one day you will understand that.'

'I do, Dad,' I whisper to myself. Age and loss has given me an insight I never had before.

'This is one of my favourites too,' a deep, sensual voice says behind me. Luis appears at my side. I don't react even though I didn't even scent him coming. My wolf seems to have accepted them both after all they've done for me. I woke up this morning to a bag of food waiting for me this morning on the patio. Breakfast of pancakes and bacon strips. It was delicious.

I didn't sleep well at all. I'm feeling much better though, more stable.

Luis stands close, probably too close, but I guess he's dressed me after a shower, so I let it slide. I thought I imagined how amazing he smells. I didn't. He smells like summer, like a breeze sweeping over the ocean.

'You look sad, bonita.'

Eyes still locked on the painting, I take a moment to process. 'The last time I was here was with my dad. We stood here and we talked about what the painting depicted. I was thinking of him.' I have no idea why I said that and wish like crazy that I could suck the words back in my mouth.

Nodding as if he understands my anguish, Luis seems to ponder the painting. 'It's the sacrifice of an alpha. The reason they are born. A burden and a blessing.' Luis speaks like he's saying a prayer.

My attention drifts from the painting to the male beside me. 'It's a beautiful piece of art,' I say, stepping back a little. This is a little too much emotion for me.

'It is.' Luis's eyes meet mine and I forget what I was about to say. 'You like art,' he states like he knows me.

Continuing my self-guided tour of the gallery, I don't know how to feel when he falls into step beside me.

We pause at a piece that I've never seen here before and I quickly observe the title of the work and the artist. The artist is Juen Tybalt and the piece is titled, *No Boundaries to Love*. It's a stunning scene, deep in a forest. A female wolf lays in the middle and two males sit around her. They are drawn like mates. All three of them.

Unsure, I stand for a while, trying to understand what else it could be depicting.

'What do you think of this piece?' Luis asks and for a moment I forgot he was there.

'It's beautiful, I'm just trying to interpret what it could mean.'

'It's of a mated trio,' he replies without missing a beat.

Head snapping towards him, I try to understand what he has just said. 'A trio? As in multiple mates?' I question, I didn't know that was possible.

'Of course, many shifter communities have multiple mates.'

'I've never heard of that with wolves taking multiple mates,' I confess and step a little closer to see the intricate brush work.

'Wolves around the world follow the tradition.' Luis sounds like he is somewhere else. 'It was a common practice in my birthpack. Diego's too.'

I process his words for a few minutes while I study the pieces.

We continue to walk quietly through the gallery. Stopping at certain points.

'Would you tell me a little about yourself?'

Not prepared for the question, I don't know how to reply and we stop at another painting. This one of a mated pair of bears. I weigh up the pros and cons of sharing anything about myself. It's been a long while since I made any kind of real effort to connect with anyone. I have Pack and I have my work. I don't really need anything more.

'You don't want to tell me?'

Looking up at the attractive shifter, I realise that I want to get to know him more. After all he did save my life and has been feeding me. 'I was enrolled at this college.'

Luis' entire face lights up and I smile softly at the boyish grin. 'Bonita, you are an artist,' he declares and claps his hand over his heart dramatically. A small giggle escapes my lips and I quickly clamp my mouth shut at the sound. That's the second time I have giggled in two days.

My action seems to have amused Luis more because he steps closer to me until we are almost touching. 'Now I know the reason why my wolf wanted to be close to you. A female of my heart. An artist like me.'

Huffing a little, I'm looking at the painting and not absorbing anything but his words. 'I haven't been an artist in a very long time.'

'You are always an artist, amor. It is in your soul.'

'Is it?' I ask softly, looking back at the painting. I don't mean to sound so sad.

That night, I got back to my bungalow after having dinner with my aunt and uncle in their den to a package on the doorstep. Diego's and Luis'

cabins are dark and quiet. Bending down, I look through the basket of goodies and touch the art supplies and sketch pads. Everything smells like summer.

Emotions rolling, I pick up the basket and bring it inside with the intention of returning it all to Luis tomorrow.

That's not who I am anymore.

Chapter Thirty One

Present Day

It's late afternoon when I get back to Farrowline. I still had a mountain of work to do after my lunch break with Luis but Tobias asked me to be here to run perimeter for Dom. He and Delfina need to go to the city for something tonight. Delfina is good friends with the leopard beta, Layken Burcher. I think it had something to do with an event he invited the pair to. I didn't ask.

I'm not normally asked to come and do patrol and while I have a feeling it's just my brother's way to get me back to pack, I do my duty and be here.

Slowing as I head into the massive, open clearing designated to the dominants of Farrowline, a smile plays on my lips at the show everyone is watching.

There are over fifteen males and females watching, their mouths hanging open at the pair training together in the middle of the space and I don't blame them.

Gilly is in the centre of a small sectioned-off area, blind-folded, ears covered in noise-cancelling headphones, standing like a gorgeous statue. Her hair flies around her back and there is a soft grin on her face. She doesn't move an inch despite the fact that Oliver is stalking around where she stands. His gaze full of his wolf. His eyes locked on the female who I know owns his heart.

It came as a complete shock when these two mated a month ago. Nobody saw it coming. The pair have known each other their entire lives and had always been exceptionally close, as friends. Gilly was in a committed relationship for a long time with another member of pack. It didn't matter though. I truly believe that Gilly needed to go through the shit that she went through. She needed to discover who she was before she realised that Oliver was hers. I've loved watching them grow and get to know each other on a different level. They're still in their 'honeymoon' stage. To outsiders, it might seem weird that Oliver is stalking her like she is his prey right now but I know different. Gilly learnt a great deal when she went to Coltonline and helped their pack find out what happened to their missing Alpha. I was deeply distressed finding out about the situation Gilly was placed in. However, she has grown so much and not just into her power as an exceptionally gifted tracker but as a dominant female.

Oliver stops to the side of his mate. His movements silent. There is a heartbeat. Two. Then he moves.

Flying at the shorter female, Oliver holds nothing back as he 'attacks' her. The male is one of our best fighters. He is a leader of Farrowline for a reason, so I understand why there is a collective tension that fills the air as every watching dominant instinctively prepares to defend the beloved female. Their protection is not needed though.

Oliver moves, his intention clearly to grab Gilly, but the moment he gets to her, she is gone. Standing a few feet away, her grin is now turned up a notch and I can see her perfect white teeth as Oliver dives for her again, his growl filling the clearing. Again, she is gone. Over and over, the pair dance like this. He moves and she has already stepped aside, dodging his advances, every time. Watching Gilly is hypnotising. She seems to know what Oliver is about to do before he does and he's not able to touch a hair on her body.

They continue like this for a few minutes and a mighty wolf leaps from the trees, his mighty paws aimed at Gilly's back. Oliver advances on her front at the exact same time and even I hold my breath and then chuckle when the males collide with each other and land in a heap on the forest floor. I didn't even see Gilly move. With only her nose, she was able to sense where her attackers were and time her movements perfectly.

Oliver and Jax shift and crack up laughing and I watch as Oliver jumps to his feet and sweeps Gilly off hers. She still has the blind-folded and headphones on and the way she holds out her arms the moment he rises, laughs softly and throws herself at her mate just reinforces how talented she is.

The dominants watching are clapping and cheering our amazing Tracker and the group begin to chat away loudly, giving the mated pair a moment of privacy as they practically dry-hump in the clearing.

'She is very exceptional.'

Side-eying the male who steps up beside me, I'm momentarily stunned by the feeling that grips my chest when I lay eyes on Luis or Diego.

'She is,' I agree instantly, exceptional is exactly what Gilly is. 'Did you enjoy seeing the city today?' I ask, just to fill the silence that has descended on us.

'Oh yes,' he grins and I forget my own name at the sight. 'This place, your pack, they're truly amazing. I can understand why you needed to come home to them.'

'That isn't what you said in Rhiattline when I told you I was leaving, Luis. Or what you implied at lunch about me being different.'

'We are your mates, bonita. Hearing that you were leaving and that you wouldn't stay until we all had time to discuss our plans was hard.' There is no emotion in Luis' voice, which is so unlike him. 'Seeing you here is like meeting you again, and it is difficult.'

Again, he is highlighting how *different* I am and how he doesn't know me. It hurts my fucking feelings, if I'm being honest. 'I have a perimeter run to get to.' I don't want to have this conversation with him now, the café was enough emotion for one day.

'I will come with you,' my supposed 'mate' says.

'Luis—'

'Nicolette,' he cuts me off, those grey eyes boring into mine. 'I'm coming on your patrol with you. Nothing you say will change that. You might not be ready to accept what we are, but you are mine to protect and that is what I will do.'

I don't say another word and shift where I stand. The world explodes in colour my human eyes can't see and I try to breath in the scents of my home, except all I can smell is summer and ocean and sunshine. Luis's wolf is a monster of a beast, so ignoring him is hard, but I do my best.

Chapter Thirty Two

Nicolette in Rhiattline

'You don't have to knock, amor, just come straight in,' Luis calls from inside his bungalow and I step into the place.

I can't see him from the door. The cabin is like mine and Diego's. Studio dwelling with a living area, kitchenette, a monster sized bed nestled beside the wall. Everything is whites but unlike Diego's and mine, it is full of colour and there are musical instruments everywhere. There's a record player playing music in the corner and on the table is a stack of albums. His guitar has been placed on the bed and there are several other instruments strategically placed around the bungalow. That's not what has my attention though. In the corner of the room is a large easel holding a big piece of heavily textured paper. Bottles of paint and a stack of canvas litter the corner.

Still carrying my box of goodies, I step over to the fresh drawing he is creating and try to control my wonder. It's stunning. A landscape of

Rhiattline in a way that I've never imagined. He's used charcoal and it is truly stunning.

'You like?'

'Yes,' I whisper, getting a little closer to view the detail. 'You have captured this place perfectly, and your detailing here.' I point to the left side of the image. It looks like a picture and not a drawing. 'Luis, it's beautiful. You're truly gifted.'

'Thank you.' Luis is beside me now, but I'm too interested in the drawing. I can feel his eyes on me. 'Is there something wrong with the supplies?'

Drawn back into the present, I look down at the box and up to the male who moves to the kitchenette. 'No, nothing wrong. It's just not necessary. I don't have the time to draw and I haven't picked up a brush in forever. So, I wouldn't want these to go to waste.'

Truly, I just can't stand to look at them. I haven't held art supplies in a very long time.

Luis makes a noise in the back of his throat that I don't understand. 'You are on holidays, right? So, you should have heaps of time.'

Huffing a small laugh, I shake my head and place the box on the already littered table. 'Time is not something that I have and this is not a holiday. I'm here to watch over the shifters that came from Farrowline, and my mum is a meddling female.' My last words come out more of a grumble and a curse.

Luis finds that particularly funny. 'What's your mother meddling in?'

'My life,' I offer and take a seat when Luis indicates towards the round dining table. He moves over when he realises that I'm going to comply and pulls out the chair for me before going back to what he was doing.

'Mothers are a particular gift, are they not?'

'Yes,' I agree instantly and a little confused by his tone. 'Thank you,' I say just as he places a mug of steaming coffee before me. He knows how I like it. Next, he grabs a few cookies from the jar sitting on the table, plates them and places it before me.

Luis watches me closely until I grab one and nibble on it. Like most dominant males, he is always very concerned by how much I'm eating.

'I lost my mother when I was very young. I was raised with Diego, by his family unit, until his parents were killed by a rival pack.'

That has me stop eating. Shit. 'I'm sorry.'

Luis offers me a kind smile which doesn't drop when my phone starts buzzing in my back pocket. 'You're a very busy female. I've been watching you for days. You and that phone are very connected.'

Unlike when everyone else at Farrowline comments on how much I work, I don't hear the judgement from Luis. Shrugging, I leave my phone where it is. 'I have a lot of work to do.'

'Even when you're on holiday? Sorry, I forgot, you're here because of your mother and your packmates,' he corrects, one eyebrow raised in question. I'm momentarily blinded by his beauty. The wolf under my skin stretches as if she is waking up, ready to have some fun with this male. Heat grows in my core.

Shoving the feeling away, I refuse to give in to the beast's desire. I don't think it'd be a good idea to go there with this shifter. I'm a very sexual female who takes what she wants, this however, might not be a good idea.

'My work doesn't take holidays,' I state and rise. 'Thank you for the coffee Luis, but I should be heading back to my cabin. I have—'

'A lot of work to do,' Luis says, cutting me off. He's all lazy smile and cocky attitude. The way he's studying me has me uncomfortable and I go to leave without another word. 'Meet me for dinner tonight. On the sand. I'll cook my famous paella and we will try and make this a holiday. Maybe have some fun. It is no secret that we are attracted to each other. I can scent your wolf and I know you can scent mine. What do you have to lose? You'll be gone soon, no?'

Stopping, I turn slightly, having sensed exactly what he means. He clearly wants me, his wolf isn't quiet and I know he's just as hungry to taste as I am.

It's been a while since I felt the skin on skin contact of a sexual partner. Pros and cons swirl around my mind. One after the other. I have rules that I follow. Rules that keep pleasure, pack, and work, very separate. The thing is, I don't know where Luis stands in all those rules. The male has seen me naked already. I'm pretty sure he has seen me throw up when I was sick.

Luis waits for me to decide and heavens help me, I really, really want to bite him, so I say, 'Okay.'

What's the worst that could happen?

Chapter Thirty Three

Nicolette is in Rhiattline

I DEBATED WHETHER OR not I should have accepted Luis's invitation. His words have been playing around in my mind. The request to share a meal tonight has a double meaning. Sex with the male next door might pose a problem. I've always made a point to not get involved with anyone too close to my 'world'. That means no one in Farrowline, not that there are any options there, no one at the office, and no wolf shifters from packs such as Rhiattline.

I know why Mama has sent me here with the others, it has nothing to do with making sure that they're all safe on this trip. I firmly believe that I'll never find a mate, because frankly, I don't want one. I have no time for nonsense and mating bonds. The mating dance has always seemed like a massive drama that I really can't be bothered with. I watched Tobias and Ridley. Delfina and Dom. Even Adalee and Easton's mating wasn't simple.

Besides, with the promises I made myself and my pack, I can't do that. I can't give myself to another with the knowledge that my decisions will impact Farrowline—again. I already killed my father. I left him undefended when he needed me and I can't give Mum a reason to leave us for the next life. The pack won't be able to handle it. Sara is in a delicate state with a newborn and Ridley needs Mama's guidance as she continues to discover what it means to be the Luna.

It's the smell of Luis' paella that has me change my mind. The aroma started about two hours ago and it's been very distracting. My mouth hasn't stopped watering, which is making it hard to control the beast under my skin.

With my wolf salivating at the idea of not only the food, but of tasting the male, I have no control over the decision she makes to attend tonight. That and the idea that Diego might be out there. The thought almost brings me to my knees. Two males have captured my attention and while it's insane, it makes my thighs clench together.

It is my wolf who picks my outfit. My core heats as I slip on a cute, above the knee, flowy summer dress. The fabric feels delicious on my oversensitive skin. I manage to think clearly enough to throw on a thin cardigan over my shoulders. Damn wolf would have me walk out of this bungalow butt naked and shivering my arse off if she had her way.

Lucky, I have some control and manage to check myself in the mirror before heading down to the sand. Staring back at me is a flushed face, eyes that scream how ready I am, and thick, black curls that fall haphazardly down my back. I look like a mess, so unlike myself that I nearly re-think this entire plan. Then I hear a guitar being strummed and the idea of those fingers on my body banishes those thoughts quickly.

Barefoot, I walk out the door and down the stairs. My feet sink into the sand and I feel each individual grain against my skin. The sight before me does nothing to banish the thoughts of sex and skin and all things heat as I look up at what Luis has set up for us on the beach.

A large, contained fire blazes and an impressive grill, that Tobias and his Circle would die for, sits on top with two round pans cooking Luis 'famous' dish.

That isn't what has my full attention though. It's the male sitting on one of the two logs that has been placed around the fire. Luis sits with his guitar on his lap, his eyes fixed on the waves and his voice singing a tune that has every fibre of my being shutter and stop. It is unlike anything I've ever heard before. Powerful and rich, deep and mesmerising. Luis sings of family, of pain, of an endless love he's waiting to discover. He's wearing what appears to be cream linen pants with a white hoodie that hugs his wide shoulders.

I can't help but admire the perfection of him. With the ocean as a backdrop, he looks like something out of a fairytale. That hair. The glasses. The energy of Luis Cortez has me rethink the rules I've placed in my life. Rules I swear and live by. It makes me consider what I'm doing. If I continue with this I feel that things will never be the same. That I'll be diving headfirst into something without all the information.

However, if I turn around and go back into the bungalow, I will be denying myself, and my wolf, something that she wants to explore and I'm not a female who backs down from anything I want. That's why I've made the business decisions that I have made. Why Farrowline is successful in both wealth and power. I helped build it to what it is today because I go for what I want.

Not that any of this debating within my own mind matters because when Luis turns his head, just as his song reaches the crescendo and those grey eyes lock on me, I take a step in his direction, consequences be damned.

Chapter Thirty Four

Nicolette in Rhiattline

Laughing into my drink, I refuse Luis' request to fill my plate with more food. 'Please no, I have eaten my body weight in paella. I'll be sick if I have any more.'

It pains me to say no, I devoured my first two plates. It was the best thing that I've ever put into my mouth. 'I do love it though. You're very talented,' I say, watching the male who gets to work grabbing my plate and piling the dishes to one side of the fire.

I'm sitting within the little campfire he has created. A log at my back and the other to my left with the ocean the only thing that I can see. He's even laid out a comfy rug.

'Thank you, bonita.'

Smiling at the way he continually calls me beautiful, I offer to help but get told to relax. The sun is setting and it's a glorious night. Luis has been an amazing host, keeping the conversation and the wine and food flowing.

'You were going to tell me about your life,' Luis says as he sits down beside me. I don't say anything about how he's sitting closer than he was before. I feel like he started on the other log when I first sat down and now he's right beside me, almost touching. He smells amazing and I cover my little grumble of need with another sip of my wine.

'I'm not sure what there is to tell. I'm the Chief Operating Officer at Farrow Group with multiple companies that I own or co-own. I like to invest in start-ups that are trying to do something meaningful and need support.'

Luis listens intently, his eyes focused on me the entire time I speak. It's nice. Not many shifters look at me directly, I think I intimidate a lot of them, humans included. I don't do it intentionally. I'm too focused on my work to be worried about what others think, which August has told me is the problem. Makes no sense to me.

Luis' smile fades a little when he realises that I've stopped speaking. 'That is your work, amor. What of your life? Your pack? What do you do for fun? What makes you laugh? What makes you cry? What has your blood boil in your veins?' Luis speaks with such passion.

I don't respond, only drink some more.

'I'm sorry,' he says unexpectedly.

Looking up from where I was staring fixatedly at the way the fire dances into the air, I can't help but frown at how close his face is. 'For what?'

My own gaze falls to his lips as he speaks. 'For making you uncomfortable. I did the same thing in the gallery. I don't mean to pry or push you to share.'

'You didn't,' I reassure him, but he isn't listening. I can tell by the way he smiles and pushes my hair from my face.

'I did.' He looks sad and that has my heart ache in my chest and my wolf ready to tear someone to pieces. 'Maybe if I tell you more of myself. Would you like that?'

I feel like he already knows the answer to that question. Luis moves to grab the bottle of wine beside his leg and fills my glass almost to the top.

'I was born in the region of Santon, my mother and father were two dominants who served the alpha with much love and devotion. Santon was a little territory near the coast. A beautiful environment to run in and learn the ways of the world. I was taught art and music and how to swim before it was all taken from me.'

Shit. My chest feels heavy under the weight of his words. 'I'm so sorry, Luis.'

Again, I am the centre of his attention and he brushes the back of his fingers down my face. 'Do not be sad for me, amor. My life is rich and full. My sadness led me here today and there is nowhere I'd rather be than sitting on this beach with you, drinking and connecting.'

I can't help but catch my bottom lip between my teeth. I think I'm swooning because I feel all lightheaded and it has nothing to do with the knock on the head I had the other day. 'Please, continue,' I manage to say.

'I was left to roam the coastline, pack-less and alone. Until I came across Diego and his pack. Diego's parents were healers, both gifted in their own way. They took me in. Their Alpha was strong and their pack small but united. I was welcomed with open arms. Diego and I were like brothers from the moment we met. His sister Gloria became my sister. Which was forged to a bond that we have today when we were attacked and I was left pack-less again. Only this time, I wasn't alone. Diego and I managed to protect Gloria and we survived. We moved around, staying with packs around the country. Most were with family members of Diego, distant aunts and uncles. Cousins. We discovered more and more family as we travelled but nowhere really felt like home, like pack, so we kept moving. Diego was determined to make our lives better. He studied for years through distant education. Gloria did too. I continued to make art and music and we found peace, eventually. Diego interned at hospitals and clinics around the world. He studied with shifter healers and human doctors until he was the best at well...everything.' The love in his voice makes me smile. He speaks with such passion even when the topic must be painful to remember. 'Gloria came out here for university after receiving a scholarship and deciding this would be our next adventure, we took the offer.'

I don't know what to say. 'Wow, Luis. You've lived such an amazing life. Your story is incredible.'

Shrugging, the gorgeous male hasn't stopped staring at me. 'I feel like the next part of my life is going to be even better, bonita.'

I shiver, my entire body feels as if it's been shocked with the most intense feeling of my life.

Chapter Thirty Five

NICOLETTE IN RHIATTLINE

'You're cold,' Luis states seriously and moves to quickly remove his hoodie. Before I can say anything, he's throwing the hoodie over my head. My wolf is too close to the surface and clearly he's picking up on her energy.

'It isn't the cold I'm feeling, Luis,' I reply, my tone full of hunger.

I watch as the side of his mouth curves as if he knows exactly what he is doing and what I am feeling. Luis hands are on my sides, no longer pretending to fix the jumper.

'Yeah?' he asks, his grey eyes studying my face. We're so unbelievably close. 'I know exactly what you are feeling.' Holy shit, his voice is like sin and temptation.

'And what is that?' I croak out. My throat is closing up. My heart is pounding in my chest and I'm so turned on that I might explode if I don't get the release I'm craving.

Luis moves slowly, his hand coming to pull the top of the hoodie aside. I sit frozen as he buries his face against my neck and breathes deeply. His skin on mine is unbelievably hot.

'Lust,' he purrs into my neck. His lips brushing against my skin.

I shiver again in need.

'Desire.'

My chest rises and falls heavily. I'm finding it really hard to sit still.

'Your wolf is shouting her heat at me. Say yes to this, Nicolette.' He kisses just below my ear and I bite back a moan.

Pulling away, Luis waits, inches from my face as if expecting me to say or do something. Give my consent to his touch or refuse it.

Meeting his hungry gaze, I take a moment to process and think through what I'm about to do. Should I, shouldn't I's run through my mind and yet, nothing can stop me from crushing my lips onto his.

It's all he needs. He takes my mouth like the artist he is, consuming my world and painting colours behind my closed lids as we both breathe in each other's air. Our tongues dance in perfect harmony until the sounds of the ocean and the growing night become nothing more than a backdrop to the art we create with our bodies.

One of his hands is on my stomach, having worked their way below the hoodie. They're too big, too hot, and they're against my oversensitive skin. Setting me alight. Pushing me out of my comfort zone. I have never felt anything as intense as his scent surrounds me, his body pressing against mine.

Not able to get enough, I rise, keeping my lips locked with his and straddle the male who has taken over every thought in my body. Who consumes me whole. His other hand is on the back of my head, keeping me where he wants me. Where I want to be. Attached to him.

A very male sound erupts from Luis' throat when I settle on his lap. My core hitting the fullness that sits teasingly close against my clothed centre and it's torture.

He grips my hips, under my dress, his fingers playing with the sides of my underwear. Our mouths haven't detached. His rhythm has only intensified and I barely take in air to breath.

Not that I care. I'm drowning in the ocean again. We're both completely locked in our passion, frenzied by lust. His wolf is communicating to mine and mine to his.

He is so hard. So male. When his hands come to pull the jumper off me, I almost whimper at the loss of his lips. Luis grins as if he has won some kind of battle and normally I'd slash a male for looking so smug at me but right now, Luis can do whatever he wants. I've surrendered. The hoodie is thrown aside and instead of giving me back his lips, Luis brings them to my now bare shoulder. The straps of my little summer dress are at my elbows and he takes the time to map out my neck, shoulders and jaw with his lips.

'Luis,' I plead, something I've never done before in my life. I don't even know what I'm asking him to do. I guess he does though because he pulls down the front of the dress, exposing my breasts. My nipples are hard and I'm not sure if it's because they're now exposed to the crisp night air or because of the pounding need in my body.

'Luis!' I shout when his very hot, very skilled mouth latches on to my right nipple.

I moan loudly, my head falling back and caught by the male worshiping my chest. Luis growls and I feel it in my core. The vibration of his body adds to the sensory overload of this moment. My dress is bunched around my middle. Luis hand is on my arse, caressing and squeezing and I sit up a little to give him better access. He growls again and this time I know he's barely containing his beast.

Realising that he might need more encouragement that I want this, I grip his face, being careful of his glasses and pull his head from the breast he is now devouring. 'Luis, I want this. I want all of this.'

His grey eyes are no longer human, they're dark and bright.

Gorgeous.

Grunting, Luis takes my invitation and my underwear is ripped in two, his hand is no longer on my arse but exploring my centre with exquisite care and understanding of what makes a female tick.

I cry out when he pushes one and then two fingers into me. Pleasure is all I feel. My mind short circuits and I growl for him to fill me.

I only sit up long enough for him to free himself from his pants. My mouth waters at the sight of the thick, hard, long length. With Luis in full control, I comply easily when he positions me just right so that when he guides me down onto his hardness, I shout and whimper his name.

He fills me completely and I need a minute on his lap to calm my raging heart and to get used to the feel of him. Head buried in his neck, Luis speaks sweet words in a language so beautiful that it has my eyes fill with water. Burying my face into his shoulder, his hands roam over my back, my hair, my legs. I don't know what he is saying but it shakes my shattered and haphazardly-put-back-together heart.

I breathe him in, using his scent to ground me, and when the moment is gone and the need for friction is almost debilitating, I move my hips and relish in the noises he makes.

It does something to me. Changes me. Reforms me. I begin to pick up the tempo and ride the gorgeous male.

Sitting up, I lose myself in the feeling of his mouth again claiming my breast and I look over Luis head and get caught in the brightest lavender eyes I have ever seen.

Diego watches us. His gaze fixed on me riding Luis. On how my breasts bounce up and down. I feel stuck in his eyes, unable to draw my attention away. He doesn't move. Just watches. His face is unreadable. His emotions impossible to understand.

My core clenches harder around Luis' length and the male growls deeply, almost pushing me to the brink.

'You like Diego watching us, bonita?' Luis says into my neck, his hands are on my arse, guiding me up and down faster and harder. I don't question how he knows Diego is sitting on the stairs to the blue bungalow.

I haven't looked away and neither has Diego.

'You do, don't you?' he prompts and I moan deeply as he tilts my hip, hitting a spot that has me shudder.

'Yes,' I say, my words barely audible.

Luis growls again and moves one hand to grab the back of my head, he pulls my head down to his so that I have to break eye contact with Diego.

I'm expecting him to be upset by what I've said but instead he's grinning like a male whose just won a battle.

'Good.' He takes my mouth in a blistering kiss that rids my mind of all thought and when his other hand comes around to work my clit, I shatter into a million pieces.

Chapter Thirty Six

Present Day

Paws pounding on the forest floor, I seek the freedom in running at speed through the trees. Wolf at the forefront, I collect the scents of Farrowline and weave through the strands as my eyes seek any disturbances or anomalies.

Jumping up and over a line of massive boulders, I hop down off the rocks with a soft thud and whirl around on the male who falls beside me.

Growling low in warning, my wolf studies the male. His grey eyes are glowing. He's almost a head taller than I am and he smells of...mate.

Emotions erupt and I lose control.

My body feels as if it's on fire and I scrape against the barrier that separates my wolf and I, knowing exactly what she is going to do.

She leaps into the air, colliding with the male and I can't stop her. Wave after wave of lust and desire sweep up my spine. Causing me to slip into the feeling deeper, making it harder to keep my head and my wits about me.

We're rolling down, twigs and rocks cutting our sides and I can't take back control. I feel Luis' warmth. His wolf curled around me, nuzzling my neck. Breathing me in. My wolf does the same. I want him. I need him.

I don't have control over my own emotions. It's all pure animal at this point.

Fuck.

I can't…get…her…to…shift…back!

We stop just as the ground levels out and I blink up at Luis. He surrounds me. Consumes me and my wolf wants him, now!

He lowers his head and nips my neck. My wolf growls low in warning and permission. She is a puddle of useless female desire and I finally get the chance to take control.

I shift. 'Damn it!' I shout the moment I reclaim my own body. Chest heaving, I glare up at the massive wolf staring down at me. His legs are on either side of my body and I am completely surrounded. 'Luis!' I demand, my heart rate spiking a little at the realisation that I wasn't the only one who lost their mind. There is no human in the wolf's eyes, just pure dominant male shifter.

'Luis,' I say, making sure to infuse enough calm into my voice. I'm not afraid of the beast staring at me but this isn't ideal, he wouldn't like this. I raise my hand and grip onto the fur under his neck. Pulling, I force the wolf to lower its head. Razor sharp teeth and all. He growls. I do too.

We stare, eye to eye, for a few heartbeats before the fur in my hand changes to the fabric of Luis' shirt.

Staring up at grey, glowing eyes, I shake my head and sigh. We are much closer now that we are both human. His face is inches from mine. Our mouths so painfully close. 'What was that?' I snap more annoyed at myself than him for losing control.

I haven't lost control in, well…ever. Adolescent shifters always do in the early years, but I never did. My wolf and I have always been on the same page. Complete harmony. Dad used to say it was because I was a Farrow. Mum would say it was because of my stubbornness to let either side control my behaviour.

'We are mated, bonita. Our wolves don't like our separation. He is getting harder and harder to manage. Have you not felt it in your soul? The absence of our touch. The pain of being so close and yet, not together. From the moment you left us in Rhiattline, I have lived with it and having you here now and not being able to touch you and care for you…it is killing me.' I see the hurt in his eyes.

I understand completely. 'I feel it,' I confess and only because we're in the middle of nowhere and it's dark and when it's Luis and I alone together like this, I can't lie or deny him anything.

'Yet, you fight it. Why?'

Looking anywhere but at him, I take comfort in the weight of his body next to mine. 'Because I can't travel with you both, Luis. I can't leave Farrowline and be your mate. You and Diego won't be able to stay here, it isn't who you are. You move around. You meet others. You have family scattered around the world. You have big plans and a life that I can't see myself in. Diego has been offered that important residency in Claymore. That's on the other side of country.' The day he received the offer from one of the most prestigious hospitals in the world, was the day we argued about what we were all doing. I left that afternoon.

'Nicolette, we are our own pack.' Luis tsks in reprimand. 'You're our world. If you want to stay here—'

'Don't say that you would stay, Luis. We both know that isn't true and I wouldn't ask that of you,' I reply before he can finish his sentence.

'Then, we are in a predicament because I'll not leave you. You are mine, Nicolette. You are ours.' My heart constricts. Luis looks at me like I am his world and for a moment I believe it. It's more complicated than that though. Words can't solve all our problems.

'Diego—'

'Diego is as madly in love with you as I am. He is just being, Diego,' he offers as a way of explanation.

Laughing softly, I find the entire world disappears when Luis says, 'I will kiss you now, mate, if you will let me.'

I agree softly. 'Only a kiss Luis. I don't know if I'm ready for more.'

He nods solemnly and my toes curl when his soft, full lips fall onto mine. I missed him terribly.

My Luis.

Chapter Thirty Seven

Present Day

Yawning, I make my way through the back of Mama's den to find some food before I find my bed. It's late and I'm freezing. Having on a thin tee and pants, I contemplate getting into my pjs but food is more important.

Luis stayed with me for the three hours I was on patrol and he's only not with me now because Jax found us and asked if we wanted to go to Tobias's den for a few drinks. I respectfully declined and wasn't really surprised when Luis said he'd love too.

Well, it didn't actually work like that. He tried to get me to go and then he was going to come back here with me and I had to do the whole, 'you go, I'll be fine' routine. It was a little much.

My wolf loved it— damn beast.

She's not happy that I stopped my make-out session with Luis in the forest. If she had her way, she'd have ripped his clothes off and taken a massive bite out of him and offered herself on a silver platter.

It's fair to say, I'm feeling a little feral right now, so when I head to the kitchen and start reheating some food, I almost abandon it in the microwave when I feel Diego enter the den.

I'm not ready to face off with him.

Luis is one thing. His beast calls to the part of my soul that I have to battle against every day— a side of me that would love to stop what I'm doing and sit around painting and listening to music all day long. When I am with Luis, I long to be free of my life choices. I want to forget all the decisions I've made and live in the moment. I envy Luis his freedom and attitude to life, which is probably why I feel more able to handle the depth of my feelings for him.

Diego, on the other hand, he is—well, the complete opposite. He challenges me on a different level. There is nothing about Diego that screams soft and calm. He is larger than life. The most intelligent male I have ever met and a shifter who demands respect and loyalty. My wolf and his clash more often than not, but when we come together, and both our walls are lowered, it is simply magic. The passion and devotion I felt under Diego's attention was like being welcomed into a sanctuary of protection and absolute care. When you spend your entire life being the one everyone comes to in order to fix problems or manage situations, it did feel nice to hand over the reins and allow him to take some of the decision making off me.

What Diego offered was a life where I didn't have to feel so alone, a life where I could share my burdens and sometimes just sit safely with Luis and be present in the moment.

But I ruined that, and I know it. I chose Farrowline. I chose my responsibilities. I'd be lying if I said that it didn't break me when I fought with the males back in Rhiattline. It tore me in two and added a hundred more cracks to my already decimated heart.

Diego says nothing as he moves around me in the kitchen, making himself a coffee. I swear these males drink the stuff like it's water, even at night. I'd be wide awake if I drank the stuff past three pm.

Waiting, foot tapping, I keep my focus on the humming microwave. When it chimes that my food is ready, I safely grab it out and leave it on the bench to cool while I find some bread. The thick sourdough smells freshly made and I make quick work of finding a chopping board and knife, all the while trying desperately to not look over at the male who has moved around the bench and is now sitting on a bar stool watching me. I feel his gaze against my skin, tracking every one of my movements.

It's taking everything in me not to jump the counter and devour him. My wolf is all hot and bothered. She needs a release, thanks to Luis.

'We should talk, Nicolette.'

'I know,' I say, still feeling Luis's mouth on mine. Still feeling his hands on my body.

'Mama has asked Luis and I to stay for a while longer and I've reassured her that we will discuss the matter with you.'

That has me look up from my bread cutting. 'I never told you to leave, Diego.' I want to make that clear. Not once since he has been here have I told him or Luis they aren't welcome. I've questioned their motives and asked them what their intentions are, but never have I told them to go.

Diego's face softens slightly. 'I know you haven't.'

'It is unfair of you to make me out to be the bad one in this scenario.'

'That was never my intention.' Diego's tone leaves no room for me to argue and I hate it. Slamming down the knife, I glare over at him. His strange lavender eyes are completely calm to my boiling rage.

'Why are you here?' I snap.

'Because you're our mate and we cannot live without you.'

Growling, I have to grip the kitchen counter and lean down to take a deep breath. My head is practically resting on the cool stone while I battle with my beast for some control. This is too much. I never asked for this and I have no idea what I'm going to do, and for someone like me, who has complete control over every aspect of her life, it's confronting.

I feel Diego move from his seat over to where I'm having a small panic attack.

'Mi amor, please,' he states, gripping my waist. The heat of him is exquisite. Suddenly, all I can think is how good he feels. How deliciously he smells. How he just called me 'his love'.

My body yearns for release.

'Tell me why you're fighting this. Help me to understand. Everything in Rhiattline was going so well. Luis and I are confused about why you hate the idea of being our mate.'

'I don't hate the idea. It's that I can't, Diego. I told you. It got too serious,' I end up saying through my dry throat.

Breathing is hard. My heart is pounding and I wish I could crawl into the cupboard under the counter and hide from the world. A thought that is the complete opposite to the female I pride myself in being.

I'm independent. I'm in control. I have my shit together and don't fall apart because of two males. Yet here I am, practically melting because his large, warm, calloused hand trails up and down my sides. The motion is hypnotic, my head is now on the counter fully.

He pulls my hips back into his pelvis and I feel his hardness against my butt. 'You need to stop fighting this. You are our mate. It is done.' His bossy tone has my core heat and I groan. No one speaks to me like this, except Diego, and I don't know what it says about me, but I love it.

Diego lowers his body so that his front is firmly pressed against my back and whispers, 'you smell like Luis, mi amor.'

All coherent thought vacates my brain and before I know it, I'm spun, lifted to sit on the counter and Diego surrounds me. His lips taste like the best kind of sin. Like the darkest parts of the ocean where mystery and wonder still live.

Locked in his embrace, teeth clanking, tongues dancing, his mouth claims the spot Luis just owned. I lose myself to the sensation of being back in Diego's arms.

It's like coming home.

Someone clears their throat behind us and I pull back quickly a little stunned that my wolf didn't even detect another shifter entering the den. Diego and I stare for a heartbeat, both panting in need. His eyes are all wolf.

I can't believe that I let my emotions control me again and look over my shoulder to see my sister smiling softly at us, carrying Nico on her right side and balancing Gianna on her left hip.

'Sara, sweetheart, is everything all right?' I can scent her distress.

'Yes, I'm so sorry. I'm probably being silly. Liam is on patrol. Nico isn't settling and Gianna feels warm and I'm just feeling a bit anxious that she isn't well and that the pup might have it.'

Gianna whines as if agreeing that she isn't feeling the best.

'I'm sorry, I was hoping to see if Diego could have a look at her and Nico. Kieran is helping one of the Tooley pups. Beau hurt his wrist playing on his scooter and I heard it could be broken which is more serious.'

'Of course, hermana.' Diego says smoothly. He gives my thighs a small squeeze and pulls away. I fix my dishevelled clothes, glaring at Diego as he strides towards the female he has just called 'sister'. He stares right back as if he knows that no matter how hard I fight this, there is no turning back for me. I am his mate, whether I like it or not.

Taking a deep breath, reason and sanity floods my system and I want to smack myself at letting the pair of attractive, addictive males get under skin. I was so hot and bothered after my make-out session with Luis and I wasn't thinking clearly. I wouldn't put it past the pair to have orchestrated this. Luis to get me all turned-on so that I'm pliable for Diego's assault.

I'm a fool. A hot, flustered and turned-on fool.

Chapter Thirty Eight

Present Day

I throw myself into work and spend the next two days focused on anything other than the two males who are muddling everything up.

I travel around North and South Sylo conducting business. I visit some of the new companies I'm helping start-up and take three tours of warehouses for potential locations with new partners. I sit in countless meetings, with some running into dinner or late into the night, which means I sleep at the office.

My phone rings and I ignore it, just like I ignore the message Diego leaves in his bossy tone that he will come and get me if I continue to avoid them.

'Roland, you know that we value you as a customer but you can't just show up at the office and expect to be seen. That's not how business works. You're lucky I was here,' I tell the bear shifter sitting like some kind of boss in the chair across from me. Roland Gromley is the beta of the bear shifters of Sylo. Bear shifters are very different from any other shifter group. They can be hard to get along with but Roland and I have an understanding, we dated a bit back when we were younger. It lasted a few months but wolfs and other shifters don't play very nice together. It was fun though and also blurs the lines sometimes when it comes to business. I knew it wasn't a good idea getting involved with the bears but Tobias insisted that we work with them on a few housing projects just outside the city. It has been very profitable.

'I know, Nic, but I was in the neighbourhood and I've been travelling for so long, I thought you might like to go for dinner tonight. I have a proposition, a business opportunity has come to light that I think you'd be very interested in. And I thought, it's been a while since we've had a good time.' Roland throws me a smile that at one point in life would have had me agree and seek out his touch. However, that time is long gone. The thought of him touching me has my hackles stand on end. The male is exceptionally dressed in an expensive tailored suit that hugs his gigantic form. Bears are the biggest shifters, only Jax could stand beside him and not look small. He's arrogant, a little pig headed, but he's a good male. Loyal. I think he'd make some bear very happy one day.

'I'm interested in your business opportunity Roland but that's—'

I'm cut off by a sharp knock on the door and then one of the poor human assistants is at the door looking like she might vomit or cry as she quickly apologies for disturbing me. 'I'm so sorry Ms Farrow, but there is a Mr Santana out here who would like to—'

Diego appears beside the poor woman, his frame taking up the entire doorframe as he takes in the office, the male I'm sitting across from and then me, the female who has been ignoring his calls all day.

For a moment, I do nothing but sit in stunned anger looking at the male who walks into my office like he owns the space. I hate myself for only focusing on how great he looks though. He's wearing jeans and a dark polo and his tanned, lick-able forearms are on full display. Diego is tall, lean muscle. He holds himself like he knows how powerful and gifted he is. Which is exactly what he is. He's probably the smartest male I have ever met and I am constantly surrounded by intelligent shifters and humans in my line of work.

'Diego,' I state through gritted teeth when I finally find my voice and stop drooling over the sight of him. 'What're you doing?'

'I told you that I was coming, amor,' he states smoothly, unfazed by my reprimanding tone or that I'm now standing and glaring at him as he moves around, touching things. Marking things, I should say. It's such a dominant male thing to do. It has a growl slip from my throat.

A small chuckle draws my attention to the bear shifter grinning at me like I'm the funniest shifter he has ever seen. 'Right, that explains it,' Roland states, clearly amused by this situation. The bear rises and turns from me to offer his hand to the wolf shifter walking up to my desk. The pair size each other up. 'Roland Gromley.'

'Diego Santana, Nicolette's mate.'

My next growl is full of aggression, what the fuck is he doing! Roland laughs loudly and takes Diego's hand. I could honestly jump the desk and claw the wolf puffing out his chest like some kind of wild beast.

'Good luck with this one, brother,' Roland tells Diego who nods his head in agreement.

My claws come out and cut into my palms.

The bear bends to grab his belongings from the table, throws me a wink and tells me to have fun and call him to discuss the business proposal later in the week.

I watch Roland leave quietly and then turn to the male now sitting on the chair across from me, his right ankle resting on his knee in a pose that makes me want to smack him and maybe straddle him and demand he takes me.

'Why don't you piss in the corners of my office next time, Diego!'

'If that is what it would take to make sure that everyone knows that you are mine and Luis', then I will.' He doesn't miss a beat. His smooth, easy reply has my lips purse so tightly that I get a cramp in my cheek.

'What're you doing here?'

'I told you that if you continued to ignore our calls and not come to den, then I'd come to you, so here I am.' He opens his arms wide to show me that he is sitting here, like promised.

'I can't do this with you now, Diego. I'm busy.'

'Yes, that is what your mother warned me you would say.'

Jaw hitting the floor, I sit heavily in my chair and glare at him. I need to get control. I need to calm down and not let him get under my skin. That is what Diego does. He seems to sneak past my defences and overwhelm me before I know what has happened.

Chapter Thirty Nine

Nicolette in Rhiattline

Distracted and reminiscing the way Luis's body felt against mine. Of how he took me and had me climaxing multiple times before finding his own release. Of how he forced me to drink some water once we were done and waited until my breathing became stable before pouncing on me again and taking me hard against the covered sand. We had sex four times under the stars with the water crashing against the shore and Luis treating my body like some kind of sacred temple before he carried me to bed.

I've never been touched like that before.

My skin is still so sensitive, I had to slept in a sports crop and underwear.

I stand looking out the window at the ocean feeling a heat in my core that doesn't seem sated. My wolf wants more. She wants everything. Luis had to head to a patrol shift with the Alpha of Rhiattline before the sun rose. I woke with his head between my legs, his tongue working some kind of magic that I think I have been spelled with.

The sun peaks over the top of the blue horizon, it's colours adding to this dream I have found myself in. It doesn't matter that deep down I know that this could become very dangerous for me. I can still see Diego in my mind, watching me ride Luis when I close my eyes and remember last night. It doesn't take away from what Luis and I shared. It turns me on harder. Confuses me.

As if I've summoned him by my dark thoughts of two hard, strong bodies against mine, Diego appears at the shoreline. I can't understand how two males can look so different and yet be the most attractive individuals I've ever seen. Diego is taller and leaner. He stands on the shore as if challenging the day to be anything but a good one for him and the shifters in his small pack. After hearing the story these males have shared, I find myself looking at them differently, especially Diego. I feel like I understand the pain and while I'm glad that they had each other, it makes me sad. Lonely.

Trying to focus on what I was doing and not just standing in the kitchenette, I get to work filling the kettle and putting it on.

I need coffee today after only getting a few hours of sleep. I'm supposed to head into the pack for some event the females are putting on for Diego's sister. The mating ceremony is in a few weeks.

Putting the mug on the counter and using the crappy instant stuff that I found in my cupboard, I go back to staring out the window. My body screaming at me to allow the memory of last night to consume my thoughts. I want to replay each touch, each orgasm. Which means I'm not paying attention when the kettle boils and I pour the scolding liquid into the mug and completely miss the mark. Boiling water spills everywhere but mostly on the hand I have holding the mug handle.

I scream in both shock and pain and drop the kettle, hot liquid flies everywhere, my half naked body cops it in numerous spots. My foot cops it the most as the kettle falls to the ground. I hop up and down shouting. I hit the mug off the bench and it crashes to the ground and breaks. All the while, I curse my stupidity and rush to the sink, stepping on shards of mug as I go.

Shaking with the adrenaline, and pretty sure I'm bleeding and have some pretty serious burns, I'm trying to get the tap on when the front door is bashed open and Diego is filling the opening.

I freeze. My wolf whimpers annoyingly like she is glad to see him and I watch as he quickly takes in the scene. His eyes scan the floor and the bloody prints I just noticed too and then his focus settles on me.

I swallow under the intensity of it and become very aware that I only have on a crop top and my underwear.

Standing at the sink, clutching my hand to my chest, I watch emotions flash over his face before it settles into the very healer expression, calm and cool, ready to do what needs to be done.

I don't say a word as Diego moves quickly and efficiently through the bungalow, being careful of the broken pieces of porcelain until he is standing beside me. He has the water running cold in seconds and gently grabs my wrist and places my burnt hand under the running liquid.

My pounding heart calms instantly with him beside me. His scent fills my lungs and I know instinctively that I can relax. That he is here to look after me, which is probably why my stupid bottom lip begins to wobble. I realise that I have tears dripping down my face with a horror that makes them fall faster. I never cry. Like ever. And if I do, it is on my own. Not in front of some male I barely know and who makes me all hot and bothered.

'Keep it under the running water for now. I'm going to go and get my bag and we'll get this all cleaned up.' His voice is so tender, so reassuring that I can only nod. I'm afraid if I speak, I'll weep. Diego says nothing of my behaviour, he just runs a single finger down my cheek in a calming gesture I'm sure his wolf has forced him to do.

He leaves as quickly as he came and I try desperately to wipe my face but with nothing to wipe it on but the small strap at my shoulder, I don't do a very good job. Not that it would've helped, the tears just keep coming.

Diego is back in the kitchen in a matter of minutes and is opening up his medical bag and laying out all different kinds of equipment and bottles. I don't look, I just stare at the way the water runs over my now very numb hand.

The imposing male is behind me now. 'Okay, we're going to leave your hand under the water while I see to your foot. I'll make sure there's no shards lodged in your skin and then assess the damage.'

I know he's only telling me so that I don't freak out when he starts to touch me. Dominant wolf shifters can be a little unpredictable when we feel cornered, but my beast's feeling very safe and content to let this male touch her. I don't look too hard at what that means. Not when I still smell Luis on me.

Diego crouches down. His hands are firm and calloused as the run down my bare leg and I become very aware at how close his face is to my core. I'm practically naked.

He lifts my foot so that my knee touches the bench under the sink and places it on his bent thigh. His bag is beside him and I contort my body a little to be able to see what he's doing. His brow is all furrowed as he inspects the small cuts. I can see some of the mug sticking from my skin. One cut looks pretty deep, the others superficial. There is a fair bit of blood but as he starts to use a bandage to clean the area, I know that it's not too bad.

'I'll need to remove these little pieces and patch these cuts up, are you okay standing? Do you feel lightheaded?' Sharp lavender eyes shoot to my face, waiting for me to give an honest answer.

Having him in this position is making my head feel a little light but I don't think he means it that way.

'I'm okay,' I whisper. My throat feels all thick and the tears that haven't stopped streaming down my face are starting to speed up in intensity. I don't know why but having Diego ignore my little burst of emotion is making me cry harder. It's so kind. He can clearly see that I'm in a vulnerable position and that I don't want it mentioned, but the fact that he is giving me this respect is wreaking havoc on my emotions right now.

Diego voices everything he's doing as he does it. He removes the pieces in my foot and cleans each cut with care and attention. My hand is still under the water and the burnt spots on various parts of my body are starting to hurt badly.

Chapter Forty

Nicolette in Rhiattline

'Are you hurt anywhere else?' Diego asks in a very 'doctor' voice.

'Um,' I have to clear my throat. He's staring at me from his position kneeling on the floor and it's messing with my head. His hair is so dark, it's styled in a way to suggest that he just woke up. 'The boiling water hit me in a few places.'

'Where?'

Not waiting for a response and with my foot wrapped and no longer needing his attention, Diego methodically works his way along every inch of my body looking for burns. He checks out my other foot and mumbles in outrage at whatever he sees.

'I'm going to spread this salve over the places I find. It may sting at first but then it'll soothe the burns.'

'Okay,' I reply weakly and hold my breath as his hand moves to my burnt foot and adds the salve. He then traces each leg, rubbing small dollops of the sweet smelling stuff onto various areas. His face is in line with my underwear next and with my lungs protesting that I breathe, I close my eyes and try to focus on the pain in my body and not the pounding need assaulting my senses.

I have no idea what is wrong with me and put it down to the way Luis left me all hot and bothered after his mouth had his wicked way with me.

Diego stops his inspection and I find myself looking down into his eyes, his hands on my practically bare hips, his face so close to the area screaming for his touch. His eyes flash darker, his wolf at the surface and I forget what happened and why we are both here.

Diego rises without breaking eye contact and I almost pass out. He turns off the water and gently grabs my wrist to bring my hand between us. As if it pains him to do it, Diego finally looks at my burn. He studies it while I silently hyperventilate and then he leads me over to the round table and helps me to sit.

He keeps my injured hand in his and sits across from me. With my silly tears dripping down my face, I watch as he silently rubs salve on my hand. I wipe my cheeks roughly with my good hand, hating my behaviour.

'Everything is okay now, Nicolette'

'I haven't...I don't know why,' I stutter, unsure what I'm trying to say. I want to explain why I'm acting like this, even though I don't know the answer.

'You don't have to explain your emotions or why you're feeling them. Not to me, and not to Luis.'

Diego is focused on my burn and I find I can breathe while his attention is on something other than me. 'I'm not normally this clumsy.'

'Good,' he replies to my hand as he carefully bandages it. 'I was beginning to worry that this is a habit that'll keep me up at night. I was afraid I'd need to start protecting you from yourself.'

What? I don't know how to take that and just sit processing what it could mean. It is not something you say to a female you don't really know.

We sit in silence for a moment and I watch him work. There is something about the way he focuses on me. Something about his hands on my skin. It makes me shiver.

Diego looks up sharply and frowns. He gets up and grabs the throw from the bed and comes back to wrap it around my shoulders.

'Thank you,' I mumble, fixing it around me as best I can with one hand.

'You're welcome.' He goes back to healing me.

Unable to keep quiet and needing to fill the space, I end up blurting, 'can I ask you something?'

His reply is a small sound in the back of his throat.

'My aunt said that you and Luis aren't going to stay here in Rhiattline and Luis last night told me that you move around a lot. Will you continue to roam now that your sister is here with her mate?'

Diego doesn't reply right away. He's now working on finding the right bandage. My hand feels amazing. The burning sensation has disappeared.

'We haven't decided on what to do. Luis likes it here for now and Gloria will take a while to settle into this new pack. We won't leave her until we know that she's secure. I won't make a decision until I know it is the right one. We don't move around until we feel the call to. Our main focus is always about the security of our family unit.'

It's in that moment that I see a little of myself in Diego.

'Luis told me...he told me a bit about your lives. Luis speaks so highly of you and the decisions that you made to care for him and Gloria,' I venture, needing to break through the exterior that Diego puts out into the world. Maybe wanting to poke at it a bit to see if there are other layers, like there is for me. Ones that others don't get to see.

'I do what needs to be done.'

I can't help but smile sourly. 'I understand completely.'

Diego's eyes are no longer on my now bandaged hand. They stare at me like he can read my deepest secrets in the depths of my eyes. He studies me, pulls me apart. 'Yes, I think you do.'

That has everything in me still. 'Responsibility is the burden of dominant wolf shifters like us. Not that we'd change it.'

'I wouldn't mind changing some things,' I blurt out without thinking. Snapping my lips shut, I want to kick myself. Why would I admit that to this male who watched me have sex last night with his packmate?

Diego's head tilts as he no doubt listens to the way my heart has kicked up. 'I'd be glad to shoulder your burdens with you, Nicolette Farrow.'

A tear slips as his words sink in and I make no move to wipe it away. Diego does. He leans forward and gently catches the drop. His hand cups the side of my face and we just sit staring. We stare and my heart races. 'I'm sorry, I don't know what is wrong with me.'

Frowning, Diego searches my face. I feel like he wants to say something. 'You can't help it, it's been a big couple of days.'

Chapter Forty One

Nicolette in Rhiattline

'What happened!' Luis is furious and kneels before me with a look I could never imagine someone so sweet could make. I guess I forgot how dominant he is because right now, he is every bit a male wolf shifter.

Aunt El sits beside me gaping at the way the gorgeous Luis Cortez is fussing over me. He has my bandaged hand in his, speaking words that I can't understand but I can guess are demands for me to answer.

I become very aware that the entire pack of Rhiattline and the females of Farrowline, who are sitting close by, are staring in shock and curiosity.

I've been here for a few hours at the back of the Alpha of Rhiattline's den, which is mostly just thick forest surrounding a large clearing for gatherings. The females put on a small event for Gloria and when it finished it turned into the entire pack coming together for dinner. I've spent the entire time out here under the trees with El and some of the other females.

I won't admit it to myself but I've been looking around to see if Luis or Diego will come. Aunt El asked me before who I was waiting for and I brushed it off. Now, I guess the cat is out of the bag because Luis is making no effort to hide that we have become 'close'. He's practically covering me with his body as he runs his hands down my arms and then sits back to see that my foot is also bandaged.

'Mierda! What happened?' I don't need to be fluent to know that Luis has just cussed.

'I'm fine, Luis,' I state and try to remove my foot from his grasp. He doesn't let me and I look over at the Farrowline females openly gawking at what is happening. It rubs me the wrong way mostly because I can only imagine what they're thinking. Probably that I never let anyone touch me like this or that I'm not clawing the male for being so forward.

'Luis!' I say louder and finally get his attention. 'I'm okay. I hurt myself in the bungalow but Diego came and patched me up.' That seems to calm him a little. 'Please, get up,' I encourage and try desperately to not take any notice of our audience. He complies reluctantly.

'Luis, she said she's fine,' Gloria says as she steps up and greets her brother. Luis doesn't seem happy and kisses her cheeks twice before looking back down at me with a deep frown. Gloria just smiles, I haven't had much time to speak to her yet.

She seems really lovely though and she's absolutely gorgeous. She has the richest caramel hair that flows down her back. It's so straight and silky. Her skin is deeply tanned like her brother's and she has the same accent and high cheekbones. Her mate is just as lovely. A less dominant male who came around with some cocktails that he made when we first showed up.

He seems absolutely devoted to her, and knowing the story of her life, I'm very glad she has found someone to love her.

'You'll get used to the fussing,' she tells me and the comment takes me off guard. It implies that she believes there's something deep between Luis and I. About to correct her, Diego appears behind his sister and the pair share a few words before he kisses her cheeks in the same way Luis did.

For a moment, the trio discuss something between themselves and I just sit listening to their beautiful language.

Diego's gaze falls to me a few times as he speaks which has me shuffle in my chair as I imagine what he could be saying about me.

'Dinner is almost ready everyone, we've served everything on the table inside,' one of the elders announces to the mass of shifters in the clearing.

Aunt El hasn't stopped staring at me and I haven't stopped pretending that I'm fixing the bandage on my hand. I'm not ready for the questions. Everyone starts to move in groups toward the den which saves me from her scrutiny for a moment.

'I'll get you something to eat, bonita. You stay seated and off that foot,' Luis states and my heart skips when he kisses the top of my head.

Aunt El chokes on the mouthful of wine she just threw back and I glare at the Farrowline females who collectively start to cough. They all shut up and quickly hop up to get some food.

That's when I realise that Diego is still watching me with those too knowing eyes. He leads Gloria away after she declares that she is hungry. She throws me a wink over her shoulder as she goes, clearly she could feel my discomfort. I instantly love her.

Aunt El opens her mouth and I quickly jump in to hurry-whisper a, 'don't say a word.' My aunt slowly clamps her lips together, the ends kicking up a little. Her eyes are sparkling and I want to disappear into the trees and never come back out. 'And not a single word to my mother or my brother, Aunt El.' I don't think she'll keep this to herself so I add, 'please.'

That has her smile fade and her brow furrow seriously. 'I promise, sweetheart.' She reaches out and grips my good hand. 'Have some fun, Nic. I want this for you.'

My hands are shaking slightly when she pulls away and tells me she'll be back with some food that I almost spill my wine when I bring it to my lips. Everything feels off, like I'm standing at the edge of something massive and I'm too afraid to jump.

Chapter Forty Two

Nicolette in Rhiattline

'I don't understand.'

Rolling my eyes is involuntary and I finally manage to pull my shoes off with only one good hand. I throw it to the side of the bungalow and eye the male who is removing his jacket and making himself very comfortable in my space. The sun is still setting, I left the barbecue early to escape the awkwardness between me and the Farrowline females who kept watching me interact with Luis and Diego. I know that any minute now I'm going to get a call from someone back in Farrowline questioning me.

'All I'm saying is that there's no need to be so affectionate when we're around the others. Especially my aunt,' I say, not sure how else to put it.

Luis is rummaging through the fridge and honestly, I don't know what he's looking for because there is nothing much in there. Which is exactly what he says after he makes a deep unsatisfied noise in the back of his throat. 'I'm going to go and grab some food from my cabin. I'll be right back,' he informs me as he heads to the door. He didn't even acknowledge what I just said to him.

'Luis,' I state, a little exasperated and then I'm caught off guard when he stops and looks at me from over his shoulder. His glasses are a little tilted and his hair is all messy.

Luis waits patiently and I forget what I was reprimanding him about. I've never had anyone look at me like the way he is. Like he'd stand there all day, staring and waiting for me.

'Never mind,' I say softly, unsure what the feeling in my gut is. Like butterflies, they start fluttering around when Luis smiles and winks before he leaves. Rubbing the space between my breasts when a weird sensation blooms under my skin, I don't notice Diego leaning on the doorframe until he clears his throat.

I nearly jump out of my skin. My damn wolf didn't even warn me he was there.

Smirking, Diego unfolds his arms when I ask him what he wants and watch as he steps into my space.

'I'm just checking to see how you're burns are feeling.'

'Fine, I guess,' I state, forcing myself to focus on my bandaged hand and not the way my wolf stirs under my skin painfully when his scent fills the bungalow. It hits me hard.

I try desperately to control my scent and end up clamping my mouth shut and only nodding when he begins to ask me if it's okay for him to check my wounds and then tells me to sit on the bed.

I comply and make a point of not reading too much into the reason why I listen to this male so much. I should show him my canines and tell him to fuck off. It must be because he's a healer and I was always raised to respect healers.

I watch quietly as Diego unwraps my bandaged hand and then examines the red, slightly blistered skin. Leaving me free to examine his face up close. Heavens, he is gorgeous. Sharp features and thick hair that my wolf wants me to run my fingers through. It looks pretty good and he seems to think so because he doesn't go to put the bandage back on.

'The salve worked well. The rest of the blisters should be gone by tomorrow.' He looks up and catches me staring and I awkwardly avert my eyes. I can feel him staring.

'Thank you,' I state as calmly as I can. My heart is racing a little and I need to focus on controlling it so that I don't give away how much his presence affects me.

His lavender eyes bore into mine when I accidently look up. His face is so close to mine and for the second time in a day, I wonder what it'd be like to kiss him. To feel those lips on mine and wonder how different they would be to Luis'.

Luis walks back into the bungalow and my gaze snaps straight to him, Diego and I are close, really close, and I worry for a moment about how Luis will react. The male just whistles a merry tune as he walks through my bungalow with his arms full of food. It doesn't seem to matter that we just ate at the barbecue.

'You are uncomfortable,' Diego says and I look back at him to understand his tone. His wolf is giving nothing away. If he is as affected about being this close he doesn't show it.

Chapter Forty Three

Nicolette in Rhiattline

I TRY AGAIN TO talk to Luis about not being so affectionate around everyone but end up falling into bed with him again and having another wild night of endless orgasms.

The pink bungalow is no longer so cold and lifeless, Luis is there when I wake up and holds me while I sleep. I watch as he paints and plays music and sings to the rising and setting sun each day. Most of the songs are prayers and others are notes to the ones he's lost and the ones he's yet to find. I find myself overwhelmed by him in the best possible way.

Diego is always there, always present. At meals he sits with us and eats. He makes sure we have everything we need and every night he wishes us a goodnight and heads to his bungalow. And every night I watch as he goes, feeling guilty and ashamed that I want to call him back and ask him to stay. I'm not a female who cheats or commits to multiple partners, not when I'm in another male's bed every night.

It's messing with my head the more I get to know them.

Sitting at the back of the mating ceremony between Gloria and her new mate, Fredrick, I find myself unable to do anything but stare at the males at the front of the procession, laughing and rejoicing at the festivities. The pack has put on an amazing event. There is a marquee and a mass of round tables and chairs. All whites and greens. There are fairy lights hung in the trees and everyone is having an amazing time. I can see the females of Farrowline dancing with a group of males and females and feel content for the first time in a very long time.

I leave in two weeks and the thought doesn't bring me much joy. I asked August this morning to not call and to divert all issues to Tobias while I enjoy today. I think he had a stroke when I told him. The damn bear shifter was way too eager to ask me a ton of questions that I refused to answer when he heard Luis calling my name. I hung up on him and it probably spiked the damn males curiosity even more.

At least I haven't heard from Mum or Tobias which means Aunt El hasn't said anything. I know Farrowline is having some issues again with loners and there is a new human that Easton seems very attached to, or so Ridley said the other night when I rang to check up on everyone.

I spoke with Tobias this morning. He told me I didn't need to come home and help with the loner problem. He's worried about a group of our females being away from pack and told me keeping them safe was more important.

'Dance with me, bonita,' Luis states, appearing beside me and offering me his hand.

Unable to resist, I accept and am pulled onto the dancefloor, my knee-length baby blue dress flows around my legs as Luis spins me before pulling me into his chest. With one hand on my body and the other gripping my hand between our chests, we fall into step, in sync with each other.

'You look stunning today. Have I told you that?'

Laughing lightly, I bite my lip and nod. 'About a hundred times, Luis.' His gaze is locked on mine, our faces almost touching.

'I haven't said it enough then, if only a hundred.'

Could he be any more swoon-worthy? The music is beautiful as we sway. Some of the pack have brought out their instruments and I'm surprised Luis isn't with them.

'You got a phone call this morning that upset you, is everything all right?'

'Yeah, for now. Farrowline is having some issues at the moment and I thought I might have to go back to pack.' I don't know why I sound so sad.

Luis tenses, his eyes searching my face for something. 'I'm sorry to hear there is trouble. Do you need to leave? I don't know if I can come with you right now.' He says the last part more to himself and it takes me off guard.

Deep in thought, Luis doesn't seem to realise that I stumble a little. He has his hands on me, keeping me steady so I guess he doesn't have to worry about me tripping while we dance.

'Why would you come with—' but I'm cut off from asking because of a heat of the body that steps right behind me to sandwich me between his and Luis body.

Diego's scent surrounds me and I feel all lightheaded. When their scents combine together, it's overpowering. Like a complete picture, it's like they should always be together. Like each note of their scents is enhanced with the other's around.

They exchange a few words. Luis nods and then I'm passed over to Diego without a word from the male who strides across the dancefloor to the band. Luis says something to the female on the acoustic guitar. She smiles warmly and hands it over. She must have needed a break because she goes straight to the food table.

Now against Diego's chest, I try to find my footing as he takes up the swaying. His hold is different to Luis'. Firmer. More controlled.

We don't talk for most of the next song and every step we take has our bodies rub up against each other. My core heats.

I have had more sex in the past couple of days than in my entire life and yet, my body still seems eager for more.

Or maybe for someone else to join.

The thought makes me shake my head and reprimand myself colourfully.

'What are you thinking about?'

I don't know why he has to sound so amused, he can clearly read my scent. 'Nothing.'

'Right.' He smiles knowingly and spins me around and back into his chest, where I'm caged there by the arm he wraps around my back.

Aunt El is at one of the tables and I catch her wink. I just roll my eyes in her direction and go back to trying to remember that fantasising about two males at once is going to get me into trouble.

Then the music changes and I look over to see Luis on his own, strumming his guitar and then he starts to sing. My heart leaps into my throat. Luis has only eyes for me and like when we are locked together in bed, they scream hunger and devotion. It turns me on and sets me alight.

My growing heat amps up and Diego pulls me around and I stare wide-eyed up at him as he begins to move me across the dancefloor with the other couples. He captures my attention with those lavender depths. The love song flows around us and like a magician casting a spell. Luis's words of passion and sacrifice and longing is all I hear. Diego with his perfect features, his strong, healing hands and those lavender eyes becomes all I see and I find myself falling.

'Will you keep fighting this?'

It takes me a moment to catch up and realise that Diego has spoken. 'What?'

'This. Will you keep fighting what you want?'

My mind short circuits.

'I don't—'

'I think you do, mi amor.' Holy fuck, my skin tingles. My wolf wants to lick. She wants to taste and she becomes hard to control. I'm breathing unevenly and I stare up at Diego looking for some kind of answer to whether I'm interpreting him correctly. If he is asking me what I think he is, I don't know if I trust what my body wants right now.

'Luis—'

'Luis, like me, is very aware of this situation and we know what we want. The question is, do you understand the situation, Nicolette?'

The question is loaded and dangerous. Do I know the situation? Maybe. No. Yes.

Diego stops us abruptly and I stand like a statue staring up at him and watch as he smiles a wicked grin and holds out his hand.

Looking down at it, I know that if I take it then everything will change. That this is the moment where I jump off into something that will change my life forever.

Turning my head slightly to Luis, I find him watching us. He's still singing and with a small incline of his head, I know that what I do now isn't a betrayal.

I steel my spine remembering that I'm Nicolette Farrow and place my small hand into Diego's.

Chapter Forty Four

Nicolette in Rhiattline

We crash through the door of the blue bungalow, Diego's arms keep me safely tucked into his body as we hit and bump into furniture. My pretty blue dress is ripped from my body and Diego growls when he steps back and takes a good look at my nakedness. I didn't wear a bra and my nipples harden under his gaze.

All I can see is pure hunger and need in those darkening lavender eyes and feeling very sensual, I peel the tiny slip of fabric covering my throbbing core off without taking my eyes from him.

Diego is breathing hard, he tracks every part of my exposed body like he hasn't seen it before. He makes me feel like I'm some kind of lost treasure. The way his features harden, the way he growls in approval. It has heat flood my veins. 'Beautiful.'

The only light in the room is the small lamp he must have left on but neither of us need it. Standing tall, my entire world tips and starts to spin when slowly Diego removes his white suit shirt, his tie flies across the room and I swallow a moan at the sight of his sculptured figure. Defined washboard abs. Black ink covers his thick arms and his chest. I have never seen anything as beautiful as the artwork on his body.

Mesmerised, I'm not sure if I can take much more until he begins to remove his black pants. That's when I think I have some kind of medical episode because I choke on my tongue. My skin begins to vibrate at the sight of Diego standing across the room, his body on full display. He is massive. He is some kind of god that shouldn't live here with us mortals.

Smugly and with a swagger that only a male of his greatness can pull off, he strides toward me. My heart kicks up and for a moment I feel my wolf wake to assess the threat and then I am being lifted off my feet. I instinctually wrap my legs around his middle.

His mouth latches onto mine. He controls the kiss, his hand gripping my hair to pull my head where he wants it and it is fucking hot.

Diego pulls me away and flings me onto the bed. I bounce once and then he grabs my ankle and pulls me down to the end of the bed where he kneels with one knee on the mattress.

I watch as he runs his gaze down my withering form. His growl makes me groan in need. With a hand wrapped around each one of my ankles, he pushes them apart, exposing me fully.

'Beautiful,' he says again to my centre and then he buries his face between my legs and I cry out his name.

I lose myself in sensation, in the feeling of his tongue and fingers and attention. Diego worships me like he does everything else, with precision and care.

I shatter multiple times, one after the other before he pulls away and climbs over me. His mouth licks and sucks every inch of my body until he is at my breast. He sucks my right nipple and then my left before he settles himself above me.

Panting and sweaty, I gaze up at him and my chest begins to hurt with the sensation that fills my soul at the way he stares down at me. Like I am his reason for living. It's the exact way that Luis looks at me and I find myself unable to draw in enough air.

Brow furrowing, Diego's features harden, if that is even possible, and he says, 'breath, Nicolette. In and out.'

I comply only because he leaves no room for me not to. He is all dominant male and healer right now. 'You are perfectly safe now. We have you,' is what he says and I whimper. *We. Not I. We.*

I feel water pool at the side of my eyes and quickly blink them away but he sees it.

Softening a little, Diego lowers his lips to mine and our kiss is full of promises and reassurance. He grips my right knee, bringing it up to his side and then finding my centre, he pushes into me.

There is nothing soft in how he takes me. It's hard and consuming.

I scream his name and moan my pleasure.

I come apart around his hard length and feel a sense of completion when he finds his own release.

Drifting in and out of awareness, I lay against the soft bed. He is speaking softly, his hands moving up and down my body like he is memorising every inch. I don't know what he is saying but it helps calm my racing heart.

'That was...a lot.' My tone is all breathy.

I can't find the care to be embarrassed that my legs are spread and Diego is between them still, sitting on his legs tracing my body with his hands and eyes. I feel amazing. I feel whole. It's weird.

'The night is not over yet,' he says and I sit up when I realise that someone else is in the bungalow with us. Luis stands to the left of the bed.

I didn't even hear or scent him enter.

Every muscle in my body tenses. The intensity of Luis gaze has me shiver. 'Say no and this doesn't go any further. We don't do anything you don't want. But you have to speak the words. We discuss things in this pack. We are family.'

The intelligent, reasonable part of my mind has been well and truly fucked into silence because I don't really register what Diego has just said. I'm too busy looking up at Luis who is still wearing his suit shirt and pants. The top of the white button up is open, showing off his clavicle and neck.

I'm instantly ready again and the two males growl in unison. It has me panting in need all over again.

I nod.

'Out loud, amor,' Diego demands, his hands are at my hips. 'Do you want this? Do you accept us both?'

'Just...please,' the words catch in my throat. I've never felt so exposed and vulnerable in my life. Never been so turned on and ready.

'Do you accept this, Nicolette? Both of us? Say the words out loud.'

'Yes,' I stutter. I want to ask them to be careful with me. I want to make sure that this won't hurt their relationship or hurt the feelings that are growing for these two incredible males. I know deep down that I can't survive anymore heartache.

'We have you, Nicolette.'

'We promise.'

I have to clear my throat three times before I can say, 'Yes. I want this.'

I give my consent, whole heartedly and pray to heavens that I don't get hurt. I fear my heart has been patched over just a little to much and any small shake could shatter it forever.

Chapter Forty Five

Nicolette in Rhiattline

Luis smirks and I stop breathing when he begins to remove his clothes. The similarities between the two males are remarkable. They're both unbelievably cut. Their skin is gorgeously tanned and they look to be made of stone. Like the marble statues of the past that I loved studying.

Luis kneels on the bed near my head and captures my lips. He's not as rough as Diego, his passion is sensual and coaxing. A beautiful contrast and I find I love both approaches.

Actually, I'm worried that I'll never be satisfied without both for the rest of my life.

A rumble of thunder drowns out my cry of pleasure as my back arches off the bed. Luis is at my breast, his mouth teasing one nipple while his hand plays with the other. Diego bites and sucks at my inner thigh.

I'm hot. I'm lost.

'How should we take her, Luis?' Diego asks and I whimper. It's too much.

Luis smiles against my breast. 'There are so many possibilities.'

'Oh my fucking…Ahhh!' Diego's tongue flicks over my centre.

Diego's hand wraps around my hip and dips to grab my arse. 'I could fill this.'

I'm dead. I don't know what day it is or what my name is.

'And I could fill this,' Luis says to my breast, his hand travels from my other one, down my stomach until he finds my core. Diego pulls back and Luis fills me with two fingers.

Yep, I've died and gone to some kind of sensual hell, because this is too much. I'm being punished for something. I just know it. I have a weird out of body experience and I fly high, lost in a sea of emotions and sensations.

'Or I could see what this mouth feels like.' Diego is above me in a heartbeat and he latches his lips onto mine. His tongue assaults my mouth.

I try to kiss him back. Try to keep up really and end up just giving up and letting him do what he wants. I'm feverish with need that I couldn't care what they do to me as long as they do something, which is what I hope they understand my small choking noise at the back of my throat means. A demand to stop playing with me.

Luis chuckles and Diego deepens the kiss.

The pair move around without Diego breaking the kiss and Luis removing his torturous fingers from my body.

They're building the pressure and when I try to move my hips to increase the tempo, his hands land on my stomach to stop me.

'Not yet, mi amor.'

I whimper.

They just increase their assault.

The pair are passionate lovers. Unselfish. Completely focused on me and my pleasure. I don't get a break. When one moves his hand or his mouth, the other replaces it, starting it back up again. It's too much.

'Please.'

'Please, what, bonita?'

I don't know, I want to shout. 'I need more. I need you both.' Never in my life would I expect to say those words, yet, here I am begging for two dominant wolf shifters to stop their torment and let me climax.

Instantly I'm moved and lifted to straddle Diego's lap. The power of the pair is clear in everything they do. I'm a very dominant female and yet, my wolf is allowing them the freedom to do what they want. She knows that she has met her match, in the best possible way.

Diego's back is on the headboard and he lowers me onto his hardness while I moan his name.

Luis is behind me and grips my face to bring my head to the side. His lips claim mine and his hand is in my hair, keeping me steady as Diego lifts me up and down. He angles me just right so that he hits that sweet spot that has me see stars.

'You ready, bonita?' Luis says against my lips. 'Are you okay with this?'

I nod and whimper and remember that I have to use my words when the pair grumble at me.

'Yes,' I stutter. 'Please. Now. Luis. Diego. Yes.' I don't even know what I'm saying anymore. Words have no meaning. Nothing matters except us in this moment.

Luis' hands fall onto Diego's at my hips and I'm positioned in a way that has my arse sticking out while still on Diego's length. Luis moves and I'm rocketed into a world of colour and explosions.

Diego and Luis shatter me completely and in the back of my lust covered mind, I really hope my broken heart is able to survive.

Chapter Forty Six

PRESENT DAY

'WE TALKED THROUGH OUR issues in our pack Nicolette,' Diego states from across my office desk. I scoff at the way he claims me as being part of his pack. I wish he didn't look so damn sexy sitting like that in the chair across from mine.

'I think we've done enough talking Diego. We all made it very clear what we all thought when I left Rhiattline.' I pick up some paper and throw them around the desk. It's petulant but I honestly don't care. I gave so much to these males. I asked them not to hurt me and they did. They broke the last piece of my heart and I don't know where the shards have gone to repair it.

Diego growls in frustration. 'You're not being fair.'

'And you seem to have forgotten what I asked you. I asked you to not...' my voice catches and I shut my mouth and look to my computer screen.

'Nicolette,' his voice softens and I refuse to look at him. I might burst into tears and I'm at the office and can't do this. Not here. 'What was said was said in passion and anger. Luis and I regret everything and I'm sure you regret the words you spoke, but we are mates. You can ignore us as much as you like, but we aren't going anywhere. You could send us away and we'd still be in your heart.'

I don't go back to den until the afternoon after Diego showed up at my office and the only reason I do is because Tobias rang and 'told' me I had to. Normally I'd ignore his alpha demands but I have been feeling a little unsettled being away from Luis and Diego. I've also spent no time with Mum or Sara in the last few days, so I head straight to Mama's den when I arrive back in Farrowline.

Making my way through the front door, I look through the mail I found on the front side table and slow at the sound of voices filtering from the back of the den. Ridley and Mama are talking quietly. I can smell tea and dinner and cakes cooking in the oven. This is home. This is why I do what I do.

Hearing Mama speak to our new Luna in that soft, understanding tone fills my heart with joy. Having this den filled with her cooking and knowing that no matter what happens, she will always be around, is why I stay firm in my position to keep things as they are and not disrupt the delicate balance of pack and my life.

'I understand that the loner issue is very important, Mama. I get that everyone needs to be safe and that what happened to Adalee at the university was serious, but that doesn't mean that I can't drive myself to work and back.' I almost chuckle listening to what Ridley is saying. Clearly our dominants are being a little too dominant wolf shifters. The Circle would never try that shit on me. Liam said something once about my staying closer to den for my safety and quickly retracted his statement when my wolf come to the surface and growled at him.

She doesn't like being told what to do.

'It's a hard position to shoulder, darling girl. Being a Luna is a great deal of work. It is an honour and a joy like no other. They will fuss over you and infuriate you until your claws come out.'

I hear Ridley laugh and I smile at the sound. Poor Ridley has been through a great deal over the last year, actually, I think life has been hard on Ridley since she found out that she was pregnant with Noah, my beautiful, mischievous nephew, who I love unconditionally. Now, she is a Luna. A position I don't envy.

Not wanting to interrupt their conversation, I slow my pace.

'Mama, I could never see you snapping at anyone or flashing your claws,' Ridley replies and I hear Mama laugh softly.

'Oh, believe me, Ridley. When I was first introduced to the Pack I was a young female with a stubborn will that rivalled my mate's. Caleb and I clashed more often than not. I hated him when we first met, did you know that? Heavens, he was the most arrogant male I had ever met. But, we were both young and full of ego. I infuriated him just as much as he did me.'

'How did you meet?'

'It was thirty eight years ago now, I was a young female. Eighteen and sent to camp where a number of packs in the country sent their young so that the bonds that tie our wolf shifter communities stayed strong.'

'Oh wow, that would have been a very interesting place to go. Why don't they do that kind of thing anymore?'

I know why, packs are too big now. Territories were owned and shuffled over the generations and Farrowline absorbed a number of packs over the years. Small packs became a weakness. Other predators entered Sylo looking for land and it evolved to what we have now. Also, I think something happened the last year that Mama went. It was the last one they ever had and it was shut down pretty quickly. I think there was a death or something. Maybe some kind of fire—I don't know. My parents never explained when we asked.

Chapter Forty Seven

Present Day

'So you met him at camp for young adult shifters?' The awe and amusement in Ridley's tone is thick. 'I'm sure you got up to some mischief. I know I did. That one time Dad sent Tristan and I to camp, we lasted three days before we were sent home.'

'Oh, we did.' Mama chuckles. 'I had all my friends and we loved and hated that damn place. Everyone came just to boast about their Packs being the best. It wasn't uncommon for fights to break out amongst the dominants and I was right in the middle of most of the nonsense. I went every year from the age of sixteen, and every year, Caleb Farrow and I would butt heads and argue. He was such an arrogant ass.'

Ridley finds that particularly amusing. 'What changed?'

'When we were eighteen, at our very last camp, there was an incident that changed the course of our lives. Caleb Farrow saved my life and we were forced together in order to survive. Fate set us on a path neither of us could've envisioned. He and I...we were...'

Leaning on the wall, I try to find the strength to not lose myself to emotions. Mum rarely speaks about Dad anymore. The other night when she was reprimanding me was the first time in a long time. It hurts.

I'm further into the den and can spy the females sharing afternoon tea on the long dining table. No one else is around.

Reaching over, Ridley grips Mama's hand. 'You were in love,' Ridley finishes for her.

'Yes. He was my everything.' Mama smiles sadly, 'and I had to find my place amongst the largest pack in the country. Farrowline have always had the strength and power amongst our race. The wealth came once Tobias took over but they were always a powerhouse in this world of wolf shifters. As a young female, I had to figure out my place. That is what you're a part of now, my girl. What I am trying to say is, a Luna belongs to Pack, just like the Alpha. Probably more so, because of what a Luna represents. What her position symbolises.'

'And what is that?' Ridley sounds a little frightened and I don't blame her. Being a Luna is a hard job, and being a human as well, I admire her. Ridley is the perfect match for my brother.

'The Luna is the heart of the pack. She is a protector, a mother, a voice for the ones less dominant. She is called upon to make decisions and looked to for help and support. The Alpha walks behind the pack, he ensures no one is left behind, he protects, and sees the dangers to our family as a whole. The Luna,' Mama continues, pushing hair from Ridley's face. I don't think I am breathing, her words make me anxious. Mama is speaking like she is making sure that Ridley understands everything, like her time here is numbered. My stomach churns and I feel instantly queasy. 'A Luna walks in the centre of pack. She knows all and sees all. From within.'

'Mama, how could I ever live up to that? Live up to you? I'm a human.'

Laughing lightly, Mama runs her hand down the new Luna's arm. 'Ridley, you have a lifetime to learn and you do everything I have just said and more from the moment you walked into Farrowline. I do not say these things to scare you. I say them so that you are prepared. I won't be around forever, darling. You are the heart of Farrowline. What do you think a pack of shifters will do for their heart?'

'Are you saying that this overbearing, overprotective behaviour I am getting from everyone is not going to ever stop?'

Throwing her head back, Mama laughs at what I am assuming is Ridley's tone and the horrified look on her face. 'Yes, that is what I am saying. You will need to pick your battles, Ridley. Let them fuss sometimes and care for you because it is what they need. However, you're no submissive. You are a dominant. Sometimes you will need to flash your claws because at the end of the day, a Luna is just another name for an Alpha.'

Having heard enough, I push off the wall and escape into my rooms.

Chapter Forty Eight

Nicolette is Nineteen

'Mum?' Pushing the door open with my back, I nearly trip on a pile of clothes that have been thrown at the door. I stop and take in the mess of the room. My mum has never been a messy female. She keeps our den spotless and cared for. Not that you'd think that with the state of her bedroom. The lamp that once sat beside her bed is shattered on the floor against the far wall and there is a hole there now that has my chest ache to see. I have been allowing Maree and some of the others to help me with Mum but I see now that I shouldn't be palming off my responsibilities to others. I have been focusing some of my energy during the day on Farrow Group and I've enrolled into some online courses that I think will help. I've already learnt so much.

I manage to find a path to the bed where Mum is lying motionless under the covers and hesitating at the sight of the mountain of plates of uneaten food. I put the tray I'm carrying down on the bed and get to work stacking some of the mess. I replace the new bowl with the stuff that needs to be cleaned. Mum doesn't move. She hasn't moved for weeks.

Mustering all my energy, I take a deep breath, push the grief from my voice and say, 'Mum, I brought you food. Some of the females made stew and Healer Kieran said that you should eat the entire bowl, okay?'

She doesn't answer, not that I was expecting her to. 'I also have some water and some electrolytes that you should try and drink.' I place two bottles beside the soup bowl and wait. Hoping that today would be different. That maybe she will respond and sit up. Interact with the world. Not just sleep and cry.

'Well, it's all here. I'll come back in a bit and maybe if you want to take a shower or a bath I can help.' I sigh heavily at the silence. 'Okay, I'll be back. I'm just going to check on Sara and make sure she is eating. She didn't have a good day today and Liam has been out on patrol and won't be back for a while yet. You should see how good he is with her, Mum. I think Dad was right about what they might be.' Nothing. 'Eat, please.'

I get half way to the door when she says, 'your father was always right.'

My entire body freezes. I have to fight back the tears before I reply, 'yeah, he was.'

'Don't find love, Nicolette. It hurts too much when you lose it. It's unbearable. Now I have to live without him. I have to wait until you are all happy and secure before I can follow after him.'

'Mum,' I cry softly and hurry to the bed.

Sitting beside her, I grip her hand and try not to take it to heart when she turns her back and faces the other way. 'Please mum.' What else do I say? 'I will always need you, Mum. We all need you. Sara. Tobias. Me.' My tears fall silently down my face. 'I need you, Mum.'

'Until you find your mate and leave me too.' There is no emotion in her tone and it scares me.

My chin hits my chest and I cry softly. Soundlessly. 'No Mum. I will always need you.'

She goes quiet again and I eventually leave the room and break down crying outside her closed door. I cry thick, painful tears. My throat burns and my head pounds by the time I hear Sara calling out for me. Her cries knock me out of my self-pity and shame. I wipe at my face and hurry down the hall to the kitchen where she is crying under the long dining table, her plate shattered on the floor and the stew everywhere.

'Honey, what happened?' I ask, rushing to make sure she is okay. She is a mess.

'I was making myself a bowl and I accidently placed it down on the edge and it all fell and I messed everything up.' Sara sobs into her knees and I manage to get under the table, crawling through stew and pieces of porcelain to wrap my arms around her and hold her tightly.

'It's okay, sweetheart. I'll clean this up.'

'Okay.' Sara sniffles and I feel instantly better when she raises those light green eyes to my face and nods. She looks so tired. So worn out. It's not fair that she has to go through this.

'Why don't you go have a bath and let me tidy up, then I will bring you some more food and we can watch a movie together on your bed.'

She smiles at me for the first time in a long time. 'That sounds good.' Sara gets out from under the table and stops to ask, 'can Liam join us later if he comes around?'

'If he comes around?' I tease and love that she giggles. 'Of course, honey. Why don't we pick the most romantic, sappiest movie we can find?'

She seems to love that idea and I finally let the mask drop when she hurries off to her room.

I get to work cleaning and making her more food. I'll do this and then go and clean Mum's room and check in on her. It looks like it's going to be another long night. After what Mum said and everything else that has happened, there is no way I'm going to be sleeping anyway.

I know that her words are going to haunt me forever.

Later that night as I sit on the couch, lost in thought, I find my mind unable to shut off and go to sleep despite my exhaustion.

That's when my new work phone chimes with an email notification and I slowly grab at it and feel my heart kick up at the name of the business who has responded to me. I've been trying to communicate with the very successful company for weeks and it seems they are interested to chat with us at Farrow Group.

It's massive and could be huge for the company. Giddy and no longer tired, I dive straight into work, loving the rush that I get from the possibility of success.

Chapter Forty Nine

Present Day

Jumping from the stool, I close the lid of the laptop and hurry to help Adalee who is struggling to lift a large pot of cooked pasta.

'Thank you, Nic,' she smiles when I manage to get her to allow me to help.

Adalee may be human but she is very much like a wolf shifter female, always wanting to do things herself and has a hard time accepting assistance. The den is full of pack. Pups run around playing, while half the kitchen is full of bodies. Following Adalee's strict instructions on what to do with it after I drain the water, I shrug when one of the elders asks where my 'mates' are. I try not to look bothered by the question, I've been avoiding the pair.

When the conversation about our guests has all the females in the kitchen giggling over their 'hot bods' is when I wish the floor would open up and swallow me whole or that my phone would ring and there'd be some kind of issue August can't manage. My life must be pretty dire if I'm wishing for problems. I need help. Serious help! Which must be written all over my face because the moment Delfina comes whistling into the space, she stops and heads straight for me.

'Need a hand?' she asks, grabbing the drained pasta pot from me without waiting for a reply.

'Yeah, thanks. No shift on patrol tonight?' I ask the female who is now following Adalee's instruction to place sauce into the pot.

'Dom said I needed to take some time and rest, I've been on patrol all day and he's being bossy.'

I just shake my head and laugh at her tone. I swear this female would live on territory lines if she were allowed.

'Nic, can you?'

Turning, I quickly help Maree find a serving bowl on one of the high shelves and then comply when one of the elders asks me to hold another bowl while she fills it with the most delicious smelling sweets.

I'm not normally around much these days for pack barbecues so I don't know why it's so surprising how different everything is. Adalee has taken control of the kitchen and everyone seems to gravitate around her, asking for advice and to taste each dish as it's being prepared. I don't know how it makes me feel and I look over at Mama sitting with Ridley and some of the other females helping the Luna organise the mating ceremony, or wedding, as humans like to call it. I can't help but remember the conversation I overheard between the pair earlier. Things are changing in this pack, good things, I think. I just can't help but worry and I don't know why.

'It's too much. I don't want it to be a massive event,' Ridley says for the second time tonight and my sympathy for the Luna helps to pull me from my negative thoughts. No one is listening to her.

Gilly, Silvia, Mama and Sara have been harassing our poor Luna since the moment they all came around and started planning. They've been at the long dining table with mountains of books and devices, planning the big event.

Ridley continues to bounce Gianna on her knee, her mouth in a pout at how everyone is taking over her mating ceremony plans. Nico is attached to Sara's chest.

'You're on my side, aren't you princess?'

Gianna squeals her response to our Luna. Turns out she was teething the other day and that's why she wasn't feeling well. From what I've heard from Mama and Sara, Diego was fantastic with the little pup. They've made a point to emphasise how great he was and I made a point of making sure that I didn't appear to care about their comments.

'No, I think Gianna would love the extravagant event that we're creating for her, Ridley. Honestly, it is like you have no vision,' Silvia states and while the tall, leggy human is a bit rough around the edges, I understand why Ridley loves her. She appears to be a good friend. If I had any, I would pick someone like Silvia. Tells the truth. Doesn't talk bullshit and seems very loyal.

'I have a vision,' Ridley bites back. 'I just would like it to be low key, you know just friends, family and pack.'

'You do realise that is a massive event, Ridley honey?' Mama chuckles and she isn't wrong.

'Please, Ridley,' Silvia begs and I continue to help Adalee.

'It's my wedding, Sil.'

'And as your maid of honour, and your best friend, *and* the event manager with the degree, *and* a job in the industry, I'll tell you when I want your input. Anyway, I was thinking we could cover the trees in the forest with...'

Ridley groans and everyone around me chuckles lightly at the sound. Ridley doesn't keep it a secret that she doesn't want a big ceremony. There is no doubt that she adores our alpha, it is just who she is. The event has been postponed a few times because of the issues that pack has had with loners, but it needs to happen. Tobias is the Alpha of Farrowline. It is a chance for our pack to celebrate, and with the hard times we have had recently, it's very important that we have the big party. I don't blame her for not wanting it though. Too much fuss.

A resounding shriek from the little boy playing blocks with Darrow on the floor has everyone stop what they're doing for a moment to watch Noah playing with his favourite shifter. I find myself smiling at how he pretends to be a wolf and smashes down the block tower Darrow has just made. I have to hand it to the adolescent shifter, Darrow is very patient and affectionate with the young pups of the pack. Something he's not when it comes to anyone else. Dominic's cousin has been through a great deal over the years. The pair begin to build another higher structure with equal energy.

Wiping my hands on a cloth one of the elder females hands me, I make my way back to my stool and open an email I just remembered I'd forgotten to reply to when howling fills the world.

My entire body tenses at the call. The den falls into silence and a mass of eyes shoot to me.

Darrow jumps to his feet fast and then stops when I bark at him to stay. My mind is already racing, my wolf on high alert as I process everything that needs to happen and everything that might happen.

My thoughts go instantly to Luis and Diego. They were both out with the dominants helping Tobias and the Circle.

'What's going on?' Ridley asks and I leave it up to Sara to explain that there are loners on our lands.

'Right! All of you stay indoors. Don't leave the den until you are given the signal. Gregor, Mark, Molly, take perimeter of the inner territory. This den is the priority. Take a few wolves and collect the others who aren't here yet.' I tell the wolves who help lead our dominants. They were in the other room enjoying some down-time from their patrols and appeared in the corridor the moment the call came through.

Another howl rips through the forest and I take a deep breath to call my wolf. Delfina is at my side, waiting for instructions. I can feel her beast's energy. The need to hunt is strong which is why I make a point to look over at Gilly to see how she is doing. A tracker hears the call to hunt a lot stronger than any other. That is why all I see is her beast as she stares at me, ready to be told to let loose.

Wolves start filing out of the den, their faces set in determination. I see them shift outside and know that everything here will be taken care of.

Stepping over to the table, I make sure to kiss Mama's cheek and explain to the rest of the den that all will be okay. Ridley is holding it together, her and Sara have rounded up all the pups and she waits for her instructions like the great Luna she is. Silvia looks like she is about to throw up. Poor human.

'Mama, you know what to do, keep everyone calm and indoors,' I address Mum and then frown when she nods and reassures me that Ridley has everything under control.

Rid stands a little straighter on that. I have to ignore the pit of unease that forms in my stomach.

Indicating for Gilly and Delfina to follow, we head outside and with a small smirk that I can't help, I say over my shoulder, 'Let's hunt.'

Our human forms slip away so that we are standing side by side with our beasts in full control.

The world fills with colour and I throw my head back and reply to the call of aid that vibrates around me. The two powerful females mimic the action and then we are nothing but violent determination and feminine strength.

Chapter Fifty

Present Day

We move as one, our breathing steady and controlled. There are multiple breaches of our territory lines. The forest is full of noise and with complete trust and focus, Delfina and I follow slightly behind Gilly as she leads us deep into territory. My wolf doesn't question that we are moving away from the sounds of battle. She has complete and utter faith in the power of our tracker.

My focus is not on the thick trees and behind the large boulders of this section. It is on my packmates beside me who are just as ready and willing to kill or be killed to protect the female beside them. I know this in my soul.

Gilly grunts a noise just as we wrap around a cluster of trees and it's the only warning Delfina and I need before we shoot forward, keeping Gilly behind us now and throw ourselves at whatever is up ahead. My wolf growls low at the idea that there are loners on our lands.

Adrenaline pumps through my veins and I'm already leaping before the bear shifter has time to spin. He drops quickly and I turn just in time to watch as Delfina finishes off two large shifters who thought they could gang up on her. Idiot males.

Delfina Knox has the power and energy of a beta. They didn't stand a chance and if I was in human form I would laugh loudly. There is no time for that though because more loners come from the trees.

Stepping back into formation, my packmates and I stand firm, ready to protect our pack.

Blood coats my tongue and teeth. I relish in the noise made by the cheetah who dared to come on our lands. With a watchful eye always on the two females holding our line, I can't help but marvel at their strength and power. The pride I feel watching Gilly move in a way that reinforces everyone's suspicion that she is a mind-reader. She moves before her attacker does, as if she has some kind of supernatural power. It is a stunning thing to behold.

The remaining two loners high tail and run the moment Gilly gets the better of her bear opponent.

However, I don't celebrate our victory.

Not yet, something doesn't feel right and I move so that I'm standing between where the loners were coming from and Delfina and Gilly.

Scanning the trees, Gilly's low growl seems to vibrate against my skin. It's no surprise that she picks up on whatever is out there before I do. I scent the male at the same time as Delfina because the noise she makes is pure rage and warning. I don't need to look behind me to know that she is baring her teeth at the male wolf who steps into our line of vision.

Cade Fletton. The wolf who declares himself the 'alpha' of the loners. A stupid title for a stupid male who thinks that he can control a bunch of pack-less nomads who pride themselves on going against what it means to be a shifter.

The noise that comes from the back of my throat is enough to have those brown eyes go from Delfina to me. The male doesn't hide his infatuation with her. From everything we know and have been told about Cade Fletton, his obsession with our packmate is psychotic.

Unable to communicate properly on four legs and feeling the overwhelming need to threaten him, I shift and throw every ounce of authority into my voice when I say, 'You break our pack laws by being here, leave now fake alpha before I end you. This is your only warning.'

Delfina is beside me in a heartbeat. Her body is close and I know that she is pissed that I shifted. I've put myself in danger. Not that it's stopped her from doing the same thing.

'We haven't seen you in a while Cade. I kinda hoped that karma finally caught up to you and one of your loner buddies finally got tired of your shit and killed you.'

The side of my mouth kicks up at that. Delfina is a force to be reckoned with and I love that she is in my pack.

'Leave Cade. You're on Farrowline territory,' I demand again. There is movement in the trees beside Cade. There is a larger male wolf watching from outside territory lines. Two of them. Observing. My hackles rise.

'Yeah and take the two other loners hiding in the trees over there with you when you go,' Gilly points to the left of the fake alpha, where I also scent those wolves, 'and the four over there,' she points left. That is news to me and honestly, Gilly is some kind of super-shifter. I guess she has the same thought about wanting to speak to this arsehole too. She is on my left, her eyes fixed on Cade.

The male wolf assess us, clearly taken back by what Gilly has just announced.

I smirk. This male isn't prepared for the three of us.

'I wouldn't do what you're thinking, fake alpha,' Gilly warns, a newfound confidence in her voice as she speaks. Cade had stepped forward slightly, making his intention of threating us is clear.

'Just a warning. You can't beat us. I'll know everything you intend to do before you do it. You've tried to best our Delfina and failed miserably, on numerous occasions. Also, you should also know that beside us now is Nicolette Farrow.' The male's eyes bore into mine. 'You're fucked Cade. Fucking run,' she advises and I hear the subtle humour in her tone.

I don't know what Cade sees or maybe he is smarter than we thought because he backs away and disappears into the trees.

After a moment of tense waiting, all three of us alert and ready for any ambush, I ask Gilly if she senses anything.

'They've run away.' She seems to take a great deal of pleasure in communicating that to us. Delfina chuckles. 'Should we follow? I can find them all.'

'We know you can find them, Gilly. That's enough for today though. Cade doesn't play by the rules and I won't risk your lives because it would feel good to rip his throat out. I didn't like the two male wolves watching either. Something didn't feel right about them.' The two females don't comment or challenge me despite the fact that they're both Circle wolves, leaders of this pack, and I'm not.

I am what Gilly has just said, I'm a Farrow.

'This attack felt different. I'm uneasy about how he ran off,' Delfina states and I can't help but agree. Something was off. Cade wasn't attacking Farrowline, he was testing us, showing off.

'I think we need to find Tobias and have a word with the Circle. Cade and the loners are up to something.'

'They're always up to something,' Gilly grumbles.

'Yes, but this time they had others watching. Loners don't watch, they attack pack. Did you pick anything up from the two in the trees, Gil?' Delfina ponders, she is deep in thought.

'It was hard to see them from where they were but they were definitely related. Brothers. I picked that up quickly. Dominant too, both of them.' Gilly's words make me uneasy. The tension is building between Farrowline and the loners testing our boundaries. I fear that very soon it is going to boil over and the final showdown is around the corner.

Chapter Fifty One

Present Day

We do a complete search of the area and follow along territory lines in a tight formation so that we don't miss anything. Gilly hasn't alerted us to anything out of the ordinary. We pass groups of Farrowline dominants doing their own sweeps to ensure there are no loners on our lands, each group stops and allows us past. I'm about to slow down to help a few shifters who appear to have some injuries when Gilly snaps a sound that has every hair stand on end and sprints off.

I follow, preparing myself for what is to come. I can't smell a threat and my senses haven't alerted me of any danger but I'm not a tracker with Gilly's power. So, I keep a steady pace beside her, my eyes constantly scanning the thick trees as we move through territory. When I realise where in particular we are heading, my feet seem to falter and I fall a little behind.

Delfina's gaze snaps to me to ensure I'm okay before she and Gilly speed off together.

I can't seem to move once I smell the blood in the air and my ears pick up on the sounds up ahead. My wolf retreats suddenly and I find myself standing on two feet, staring at the trees, afraid to move.

The path ahead, the rocky boulders and the trees are the backdrop to so many nightmares. One tree sits to the right and curves in the most fascinating way just up ahead. It's actually beautiful and was the subject of an art piece I created when I was creating my portfolio for art school. I haven't looked at it in such a long time, the art and the tree itself. I don't come out here. Not after what happened.

Closing my eyes, I focus on taking deep breaths and not let the anger of my stupid behaviour take over. I need to follow the others. Something is happening and I might need to help. It is my duty to help even if every fibre of my being is screaming at me to run the other way and avoid this place. At least, that is what I'm thinking until I smell the distinct coppery scent of blood. She takes over so quickly that I'm in the clearing that we normally refuse to go near. I'm on two feet before I can process the grief of being here and then see what has my wolf take over and thrust me back into the present.

Tobias and Dom are tending to two dominants who have been injured. Tobias is covered in blood. Dom too. It appears this is where the biggest battle was fought.

I count six injured. Two unconscious.

I watch the commotion with an unattached awareness. Jax shouts at Delfina to find Kieran or Diego because one of our females is on the floor bleeding from a wound in her side that looks pretty bad. Gilly announces that she will be quicker at finding the healers and shifts just before she disappears. Delfina is hot on her tail when Oliver throws her a pleading look to watch over his mate and if I could talk I would've told Delf to go with her too. There could still be a threat nearby. However, I can't find my voice.

My body feels numb.

I'm assaulted with the most horrific memories and I feel as if I'm nineteen again, standing in the exact spot having gone against the command for me to head right back to den.

Being here hurts my soul.

It ruins me.

A wave of panic floods my system.

I don't know what I do that catches Tobias attention but he shouts my name.

'Nicolette, go back to inner territory,' Tobias yells, but it sounds all muffled and I look over at my brother and my alpha in confusion. He is still helping a few of the wounded and in my panic filled mind, I can't interpret the emotions on his face. Is he hurt?

Strong, firm hands grip my shoulders and I blink up at Tobias when he shakes me and I realise he was saying my name. 'Nic, go back to den. Everything is all right. I will sort this mess out and then I'll meet you at Mama's. Go make sure that everyone is all right. Go check on Mama.'

I don't move. All I can see is the blood on his arms, the blood of our injured packmate.

Blood. It was everywhere that morning too. I had never seen anything like it. So much noise. So many screams and roars.

Hands shaking, the image of my father lying motionless and bloody on the forest floor flashed in my mind. Lifeless.

Tobias hasn't stopped speaking to me, he is trying to reassure me but he wasn't there. He didn't see him. He didn't watch it all happen. So many dead bodies.

'Go, Nic,' he commands in that tone that leaves no room for defiance.

I turn and run into the dark forest. Hating myself more than I already do.

Chapter Fifty Two

PRESENT DAY

Shaking, I grip the trunk of a tree and vomit the contents of my stomach. I stumbled my way to one of the furthest points in territory, deep in the forest and away from pack lines and inhabited areas. To a section of pack that I love and hate in equal measures.

I must love to punish myself.

A small creek flows through this part of Farrowline and small white flowers cover the floor and yet, not even their beauty can pull me from my grief.

Memories push their way into my mind painfully, breaking through the barriers that I've carefully constructed to keep them at bay. My dad and I used to come here and sit by the rushing water and talk for hours. It was our place. Somewhere only he and I came to get away from everyone and just be father and daughter.

I can still hear our last conversation here. It was about art school. He sat me down and told me that it was okay if I dreamt of a life outside of

Farrowline, that I shouldn't feel guilty for wanting something different. He made me swear that I would never give up my dreams.

It makes me sad to think of it because I didn't follow them. I stopped making art. I stop listening to everything I loved.

Another thing I have done that makes me a horrible female.

I just want to be free of this pain, of the responsibilities of the past. I want... I want to be back in the blue bungalow painting with Luis and sitting beside Diego as I work. I want to be fed delicious food. I want to go back to those weeks where I found myself again, in art, in laughter and passion.

'Bonita!' Luis is beside me in a heartbeat, his hands running over my body like he is making sure that I'm okay. His scent warms my cold soul. 'What happened? Are you hurt?'

'I couldn't stay there in that clearing,' I mumble, feeling numb now.

'Oh, mi amor.' Luis pushes the hair from face, searching my eyes for answers. 'Talk to me. What happened?'

Diego appears beside me in the next blink and I stare at the healer who should be tending to my wounded packmates. Even though I don't think I voiced it aloud, Diego tells me not to worry. 'Everything has been secured and all wounded shifters have been healed. When we heard you left on your own, Luis and I followed your scent. Even if there were thirty wounded shifters just behind the trees, *this* is where I will be. My profession is not what drives me, but my pack. Luis. Gloria. My mate.'

His sincerity shocks my system, rousing me from the pit of despair that had grown in my mind.

'Alpha Tobias and the Beta also said that we might find you here, that this was a special spot where you and your father would go to and talk,' Diego speaks softly as he pulls things out of his doctor bag and starts checking my vitals. He is so handsome, so unbelievably calming.

'My father was murdered in that clearing. I ran away and I left him alone.'

'Mi amor,' Luis coos, drawing my attention to him. I lean into the hand he uses to cup my face. My wolf responds instantly. It was so stupid of me to fight against the feelings I have for these two. I may not have voiced that they're my mates but I feel it. In my soul, I feel the connection to them.

When I left Rhiattline, I felt their absence like a weight crashing down on my chest, making it hard to breath.

'I ran away and left him,' I tell them.

'Tell us, amor? Grief needs to be shared or it festers and leaves wounds that cannot be healed.'

'We see how this affects you. We have always felt your sorrow. It has become our own.'

'You've heard our story, amor. You have listened and witnessed our own pain. Would you not let us shoulder yours with you?'

The pair stay quiet, allowing me time to process and decide if I want to share what happened. They don't pester me or push me. They do what they do best, they let me be...me.

'I made a promise to myself. To Mama. If I find my mates...she will...there is nothing keeping her in this world anymore.'

The words spill from my lips and I tell them everything. With Luis's hands on my body, keeping me calm and Diego's hands assessing me to make sure that I am healthy, I spill the depth of my pain and my guilt. I share with them my shame and let the fear of their judgement slip away when neither of them look to me with disgust. I realise that nothing could shock them, that they have witnessed and experienced such grief and horrors in their own lives. It comforts me in a weird kind of way. As if they will truly understand.

With each word that leaves my mouth, I feel my shattered heart heal itself, piece by piece, until I feel a little less heavy.

'Arms up,' Luis commands and I lift my arms without fighting it. The shirt is slipped over my head and thrown into the hamper in the corner of my bathroom.

Diego is adjusting the temperature of the water gushing into the large tub and I can't help but remember the first time these males bathed me. So much has changed since then, so much has been said and so much has happened.

I feel strange, like my mind and my body aren't attached. I don't even remember getting back here and into my room. Luis and Diego had to practically pick me off the floor of the forest. Speaking about what happened for the first time, I'm so unbelievably tired. It felt like each word drained the energy from my body, leaving me weak and exposed to the two males now undressing me together. There is nothing sexual about the act. It is just simply them showing their devotion to me and that is what I feel. Devotion. It is what mates do for each other.

The thought draws me back into the part of my brain that stores my memories.

Chapter Fifty Three

Nicolette in Rhiattline

For the next week, I'm treated like a queen. Luis feeds me the most exquisite food. Diego and I sit and chat and debate topics that are stupid to argue about but we do anyway. We spend our nights on the beach, laughing and listening to Luis play music. I sit in the sun and pose for him as he paints my portrait using colours so deep and vivid that a tear slips from the corner of my eye when I finally see it.

I lay across Diego on the bed and do some work on my laptop while he does the same on his own. We don't speak for hours and yet our touch is all that we need. He doesn't tell me to stop and that I'm doing too much because he's as needed as I am. Shifters of Rhiattline come to the bungalow with injuries or he gets calls from colleagues around the country to discuss cases. The only time they say anything is when they coax me to eat or take a break and it's done in a certain way that I'm not made to feel as if I'm doing something wrong.

August pesters me for information on our every call and on every call I hang up when he starts.

We have sex on every surface of the bungalow and on the beach and in the water. Sometimes it's all three of us locked together or it's me and one of the males taking our pleasure when we feel the desire. A desire that is always there. I fight with the pair every time I worry that I'm going to come between them and try desperately to put space between us and am roughly pulled back into their arms and into their bed. I can't get enough of how it feels when they touch me. I crave it. I need it, and yet, I can feel time slipping away as the days go by and the end of my 'holiday' ticks closer.

Farrowline is always in the back of my mind. I have to listen to everything that is happening with Easton and his new human 'friend' from afar. I hate that I'm not around when a loner attacked her at her university. I wanted to shift and run back to pack and kill a few of them.

Watching Luis and Diego swimming in the waves, I can't help but laugh when Luis turns around before he is about to do something to make sure that I'm watching.

It's hilarious the way Diego flicks water at him and I can only guess what he is reprimanding the goof about. He's probably telling him to stop showing off, which of course Luis doesn't listen to. He still turns and waves at me and does the little trick when the next wave hits.

I'm laughing so hard at this point that tears pool in my eyes. Damn males have gotten so far under my skin that I worry I'll never be able to dislodge them. I don't think anyone could blame me though, looking at them, half naked in the ocean. Their toned, defined, lean bodies on full display. They shine under the blazing sun. The sky is gorgeous to match the beauty of the pair.

The tranquillity of the moment flaws me and for the first time in a very, very long time, I feel the urge to create.

Looking over at the art supplies that always seem to accompany Luis wherever he goes, I reach for the sketchpad and grab a pencil.

I do something that I haven't done in years.

Hand flying over the paper, I slip into the part of my soul that I've been ignoring since the day my father was murdered, and it feels like...taking a breath.

I get lost in the piece, knowing that I'm a bit rusty and it's not very good.

'Bonita.'

Startled, I jump and look up at the male standing over me, water drips on my head and around me in the sand.

Grey eyes staring at me as if I'm some kind of apparition, Luis looks astounded. 'My heart, you're a talent like nothing I've ever seen.'

Tsking, I look down at the sketch and see every wrong stroke and flaw. 'I haven't drawn something in a really long time,' I confess.

Diego sits down heavily beside me, kicking up wet sand. 'Why did you give up?' he questions and I hand over the drawing of him and Luis in the water.

Luis begins to dry off and for a moment I forget what Diego asked me. Inspiration for a different kind of drawing flashes in my mind and I blush. Luis grins down at me like he can see exactly what is in my head.

'Nicolette?'

'After I lost my dad, I had to change a few things and art wasn't the priority anymore,' I reply vaguely. They both share a look and I wait for the follow-up questions but get nothing.

'When I lost my family, I thought that I'd never find joy in music again,' Luis says instead and sits on my other side. His words have me gasp and turn to him. The thought of a poor adolescent Luis's passion being extinguished breaks something in me. It makes me want to rage at the world for hurting someone so precious.

'For me, I discovered that burying myself into making sure that Gloria and Luis were looked after and that I was able to provide a better life for them was easier to focus on rather than remember what I had lost,' Diego adds. His arms rest on his raised knees and he stares out into the ocean while playing with the sand. He picks it up and lets it move between his fingers.

'We learnt over time to accept our grief, to speak about it even when it hurt. To remember.'

Remember. Accept.

Shaking my head is involuntary, there is no chance of that happening for me. 'I'm glad you were able to find peace. Both of you.' But they weren't the ones who killed their parents or left them to die alone. I did.

From the story I was told, it sounded like Luis and Diego fought bravely to defend their pack and left to protect their sister.

What did I do? I left my dad.

'We live for each other, knowing that we will find our mate and build our pack again even if that looks different.'

The mention of finding their mates has me pulled from my pity party and right into another one.

Sitting between these two males feels like home and yet, it makes no sense. We are having fun, the three of us. It can't go any further, can it? I know what I'm feeling is intense and unlike anything I've ever felt and I'm smart enough to have considered that one of them could be, but the thought makes me physically ill. I could never pick between them and keeping them both is absurd, right?

Unless...the painting in the Blighton Art Gallery flashes in my mind.

Chapter Fifty Four

Nicolette in Rhiattline

'Luis, can I see yet?'
'Not yet. Step. Step.'

I follow his instructions while holding the hands he has over my eyes, keeping me from seeing what surprise he's organised. I already know that we're stepping up into his bungalow. I hear the door open and chuckle when Luis makes the most adorable sound in the back of his throat. He is happy and his wolf is rubbing against my skin.

We stop just inside the door and then Luis, who is practically vibrating with excitement, asks if I'm ready. 'Yes,' I half shout in anticipation.

'Okay. Three, two, one.' Luis drops his hands and I have to take a moment to adjust to the brightness and then end up standing there gaping.

'Luis, I...' His bungalow has been arranged differently to how I remember it. He has created a space for a second artists to create art beside his. There is a chair, a large canvas, which appears to be brand new, and new paints and charcoals. A studio for two. My heart hurts.

'I thought, while you're on holidays, we could work together on some new art. You can use this space whenever you want. We're spending all our time in the blue bungalow so we can use this for a different purpose. Or for that purpose too,' Luis throws me a suggestive wink and I shake my head and stay focused on what he has done.

'Art is…it is…I didn't…'

'I know, bonita,' Luis sighs and comes up behind me to pull me against his chest. He hugs me close. 'I saw you drawing that piece. I saw the focus. Your energy was completely different, you create with such passion. It was beautiful. You are beautiful. I understand that there's pain in art for you but it can also heal you, if you let it.'

Spinning so that I can see his face, I stare up at my sweet Luis and his thick black glasses and smile. 'Luis, you're unlike anyone I've ever met before and I don't know how to thank you. Art was something I gave up but being here with you…I don't feel so disconnected from it.'

Looking over my shoulder, I process the gift that he's giving me. 'I'd love to create art with you.'

Like I have just told him that I love him, Luis beams, his grey eyes shining with passion as he take my mouth in a bruising kiss.

Laughing so hard that I'm crying, I listen to Luis give me fake praises for the shit-arse piece of art that I've just created. I'm covered in paint and I've just made something so foul that I can only love it harder. Luis exclaims how amazing it is, all the while the drawing he just did is probably the most stunning thing I've ever seen in my life.

Diego comes into the bungalow while I'm laughing-crying and Luis is being so silly and giving me compliments as he laughs along with me.

I lose it when Diego steps up behind us and tells me that it looks, 'good,' while he tries to school his tone and his face to not show his true feelings.

It's fucking hilarious and the pair just watch smiling at me while I wipe my face.

In less than five minutes, we are all limbs and pleasure and mouths.

'Is that paint on your hand? Are you smiling?'

'August!' I snap at the male on the screen who seems to think that if he presses his face any closer to the laptop that he'll be able to see me properly. I'm sitting in the blue bungalow on the round table, trying to get my assistant to focus enough to finish our meeting. I've already been on this damn video chat for an hour and the barbecue that Diego and Luis are cooking out on the beach is calling. I can smell the seafood and I'm getting impatient.

'You *are* smiling!' August accuses. 'Ohh my heavens...you're having sex!'

'August, that is highly inappropriate!'

'Inappropriate, we had a meeting once at your gynaecologist appointment.'

Considering that, I concede that stating the truth probably isn't inappropriate.

'Give me the gossip.'

'No,' I snap, drawing the line. The moment August finds out, the entire office will, which means my brother and my mother will.

'Has Nicolette Farrow found her mate?' I open and close my mouth a few times. Did he just…and why am I…I think I have some kind of malfunction. 'Well, I'm glad that you're having a good time. You needed a holiday.'

Hanging up on August, knowing that I have fully checked out now, I end up standing at the door to the bungalow, watching the males cook and feel a weird sort of tug toward them. It has me pause.

Chapter Fifty Five

Nicolette in Rhiattline

Having woken up feeling uneasy, I detangle myself from the limbs wrapped around me and quietly start to make myself a coffee. The males barely rouse, they're both so used to me getting up with the sun and needing a caffeine fix before anyone can speak to me.

It's early and my phone has been lighting up since the moment I stumbled out of bed.

Waiting for the water to boil, I find Farrowline at the forefront of my mind.

When a new message appears on my phone, I decide to answer it. Aunt El has asked if I want to head into Blighton with some of the others and I find myself jumping at the idea.

Standing before the painting of the wolf shifter with her two mates in the art gallery. I try to manage the raging thoughts swirling around in my mind.

Two mates.

I don't even want one.

Well, at least I didn't...no, I definitely don't.

I rub at my temples, feeling a headache coming along and sit on the long bench that runs through the middle of the room. You can sit on it and admire all the paintings.

I left the others after brunch and came here while they shopped. I needed to see this piece again, hoping that it would give me some answers.

Luis and Diego have completely consumed me. For the first time, in what feels like forever, I don't feel like I have any control over my own life. However, on the other hand, I feel free and grounded. It's weird and hard to explain. I feel adrift and the thought of going home in a few days makes me sick to my stomach.

I'd never say this out loud, but I don't...I don't think I want to go back to Pack. How horrible is that! I should be loyal. I should be repaying my sins to Farrowline and looking after my mum.

However, an absurd thought has slipped into my mind over the last few days about my feelings for them.

I look down at my hand. It *is* covered in paint. Luis and I had a great time after dinner last night using our bodies to make patterns and shapes while we were half-naked on a canvas that spanned the majority of the blue bungalow. Diego watched with a soft, content look on his face and when Luis and I got ourselves into a very particular kind of position, he decided he wanted to join. I laughed so hard, I gave myself a stitch.

Leaving them will be hard but necessary because the fantasy in my mind can't be real.

It still doesn't stop me from pulling my phone out of my pocket and dialling the number of the male I really need to speak to.

'Nicolette? Is everything all right?' Easton asks after two rings. He sounds worried. Our Enforcer has been very busy lately but I can always rely on him to answer.

'Yes, everything is fine. I just need to ask you a question, if you're not too busy?'

'Never too busy for you, Nic.' He is being fully serious and it is such an Easton comment to make. If Jax or Dom said this, I'd be snapping at them, but with Easton, you get what you get. He only says what he means and he is loyal to a fault. That's why he is such a great Enforcer. He deals with pack issues with honesty and firmness. It was a bright day, the day we adopted the young Easton Silas into Farrowline.

'I wanted to ask you about the painting by Juen Tybalt, the piece titled *No Boundaries to Love.*' I stare at the artwork in question, trying to not overthink things.

'Yes, such an amazing artwork. You must be at the Blighton Art Gallery. He only ever painted one piece and that was it. History tells us that he found his mate not long after. He and a close packmate both claimed a female from a rival pack. The history of their story is unreal, I'll have to send it to you.' I can hear the smile in Easton's tone, the one he gets when he has his 'lecturer voice' on. He doesn't take a breath as he speaks so passionately about it. 'What would you like to know about it?'

'What is the story behind the painting?'

'You mean the concept of multiple mates?' Easton clarifies and continues when I confirm. 'It's not really well documented but it's not necessarily something that we don't think can happen. It happens in a number of shifter communities. Bears have multiple mates, as do jaguars. It's not very common amongst wolves though. Some scholars believe that multiple mates is necessary for shifters who have numerous needs. I read a paper once that spoke of a soul so complex that it will call to multiple mates in order to be satisfied.'

I contemplate each word he speaks. 'What does a complex soul mean?'

'That's up for interpretation.' Easton is such a teacher. 'A complex soul could mean a shifter or human who has experienced a great deal in life. It could mean a soul with contrasting loves and passions. Personalities even.' I genuinely don't know if this conversation is making me feel any better. 'I guess the main point to take from this is that it not common but not unlikely. Why do you ask?'

'No real reason,' I respond a little too quickly. 'It was a conversation I had with someone and wanted a better insight.'

I hang up, making sure that he is managing and that Farrowline is doing well and sit for the next hour just staring at the painting and wondering why I'm here.

Chapter Fifty Six

Nicolette in Rhiattline

'What's wrong, Nicolette?' Diego asks for the second time and I realise that I'm moving the strips of honey chicken around on my plate.

Looking up, I tell him once more that I'm all right and get the same deadpan, unconvinced expression back.

'Do you not like the food? I can make you something else,' Luis offers and I'm quick to tell him that it's the best chicken I've ever put in my mouth. We are sitting around the small table in the blue bungalow where we spend most of our days and night.

I was going to stay in my own cabin tonight but that didn't last long after my wolf smelt the aroma of Luis dinner. My damn stomach was in full control when I agreed to come over and eat.

Not that I'm eating.

Diego is on his laptop looking very serious and Luis is painting in the corner. He has been very focused on whatever it is that he is painting. All I see is dark colours and lines. A painting I started last night sits on the floor beside him and I watch as he continually stares down at it. Something is going on here between them and I'm only now starting to understand that after I finally stop analysing the absurd thoughts in my head.

'I should ask the same question of you two, what is wrong?' I question.

I put down my fork and focus on the pair who aren't looking at each other. My mind races and I start spiralling in my head when they don't respond. What if it's me and what we are doing? Am I getting in the way of their friendship and brotherhood? This is exactly what I feared. I should get up and go back to the bungalow.

'It's nothing—'

'Maybe you should tell Nicolette what you've been offered before you say it's nothing.' Luis doesn't sound too impressed, which does nothing to keep me calm.

'What's going on?' I demand.

'I've been offered a job in Claymore, at the university hospital.' Diego's lavender eyes are set on me as he tells me his big news. News that makes my stomach drop into my chair. Diego knows this, I can see it in the way he's staring.

'Claymore is on the other side of the country,' I say like an idiot. Clearly they know the details of where Claymore is, he's just been offered a job there and this male does nothing, I have learnt, without knowing all the facts.

Claymore is a lively city, dominated by shifters who live together in harmony. Small strips of territory can be rented and owned for however long the shifter needs it. I've heard that the facilities and infrastructure are amazing. The hospital, that Diego must be referring to, is one of the best in the world. I've never been but have heard that it's a great territory filled with nature and low buildings. Not a typical city. I've always wanted to go.

Luis makes an odd noise that has me look over my shoulder but he hasn't taken his focus from his very dark painting. It reflects his mood, I guess.

Getting somewhat of a handle over myself and ignoring the pounding of my heart, I clear my throat and say, 'congratulations Diego. That sounds like a great opportunity. When do you leave?'

'We will leave in a few weeks, if we decide to go. We'll make sure that Gloria is settled and then we will travel together. If that works for us all.'

We. Us. The thought makes me sad. I want to ask him if he means me in that 'we' or the 'us', which is stupid. I look over at Luis once more and wonder why he hasn't added anything.

Stomach rolling and not sure how I feel, I mumble some inane comment that's a mix between, 'that sounds nice' and 'have fun', and comes out as, 'that's nice fun, sounds like you will have...fun.' *What a moron!*

In this moment, I hate what I'm becoming. I hate that I'm sitting around in an art gallery staring at a painting depicting multiple mates and now I'm sad over these two leaving when I have to leave in a week anyway. I've spent two weeks painting, eating and finding pleasure unlike anything I've ever experienced, and it has consumed me. I'm playing den like a pup. These males have devoured me to the point where I'm not even acting like myself anymore. Honestly, I want to kick my own arse.

'I think we should talk about the logistics of—'

I clear my throat, cutting Diego off. His lavender eyes are set on me. They burn my skin. Thanking the heavens when my phone starts buzzing, I rise slowly and excuse myself.

I spend the rest of the night in the pink bungalow and neither Diego nor Luis come to me, it's the first time since the night we all had sex that we don't sleep in the same bed together.

I barely sleep and I refuse to admit to myself it's because they aren't here with me, their limbs tangled around mine, keeping me secure and feeling truly safe.

I just end up sitting by the window, staring out into the ocean knowing that this is way too serious and has gotten out of hand. Maybe this is a good thing, I'm only feeling this uneasy because of what August said about me finding my mate and then the stupid painting at the art gallery. This is all in my head and I'm being silly. I'm having fun on my holiday. Nothing more.

I'm roused in the dead of night from a fitful sleep to two dominant males slipping into my bed. I sigh deeply, the thoughts plaguing me evaporate and with one strong, defined body at my front and the other wrapped around my back, I finally sleep soundly.

Chapter Fifty Seven

Nicolette in Rhiattline

'What? How could this happen!'

I wake instantly and am on full alert. I'm only stopped from springing out of bed by the hand Luis places on my shoulder. I look up at his grim expression and then over to the male pacing and shouting words I can't understand into the phone at his ears.

The tension and energy in the room has every hair stand on end.

'What is going on?' My wolf is on the surface, ready for battle. Ready to defend my males to the death. I pause and not because Diego is shouting but because of what has just slipped through my mind.

'Where is she now?'

'Who?' I whisper up at Luis.

'Gloria has been in some kind of accident. She has broken some bones. I'm not sure what else.' His tone has me hop up on my knees and hug him from behind. He needs comfort and I don't think twice about providing it. My own wolf needs it too, Gloria is a sweet young wolf and she means so much to them. I rest my chin on his shoulder and we both watch Diego move back and forth as he demands answers. It sounds bad and Luis' wolf brushes against my skin, seeking my touch.

Diego swears colourfully and then the phone is being thrown across the room and then he is quickly getting dressed. 'She is at the hospital. No one is operating on her but me,' he says even though we didn't say a word.

I feel Luis tense and I kiss the side of his neck and let him stand up. He quietly grabs his clothes.

'Luis,' Diego says it like a plea and I have to bite back a whimper.

'I know, brother. She'll be fine. You'll go to her and you'll heal her,' Luis states with such conviction that a single tear slips from my eye. He leaves no room for doubt. His trust in Diego is absolute and when he turns and kisses me square on the lips, I find myself leaning into his embrace. Wanting him to have that same faith in me.

'We will be home soon, bonita,' he says with his lips still close to mine.

I don't offer to go with them. I just watch them go. Diego strides out like he is ready to burn down the world and Luis follows like a solider ready to light the match for him.

The sight of them leaving leaves me with a sense of foreboding.

'What do you mean you've decided not to meet with Silasline?' I demand, not sure what I'm hearing is right. Tobias would never do that. Understanding if Silasline is the reason the attention of the loners are on Farrowline has been a top priority for every member of my pack.

'Easton needs to be with Adalee, Nic. And we need to be there to support them both.' My brother sounds like our father.

'Yeah, you do. They're mates, aren't they?'

'You know we won't know until she announces their bond.'

'I know exactly what you know and don't know as an alpha, Tobias. Dad used to say stuff to me all the time.'

Tobias laughs and I love the sound. It makes me happy.

I'm not a fool, Tobias didn't call for a quick chat about Easton and his new mate. 'How many are going to Adalee's hometown?'

'Most of the Circle. Only Liam will stay behind with Sara. This new pregnancy is taking a toll.'

That's the first I'm hearing about this. 'I didn't know.'

'She's okay, just tired and feeling weak. Kieran is comfortable that all is well, she just needs rest.' He isn't reassuring me like he thinks he is.

'I need to come back to pack. With the Circle going and Sara needing Liam, you need me to come and look after Farrowline.'

Why does that feel hard to say?

It is my duty and yet, it makes me feel ill.

Last night I wanted an answer from the universe and this is it. I'm being dumb thinking about multiple mates and staying here playing den with Luis and Diego.

'I know that you have another week until you're set to return, but it would be really helpful if you could, Nic. With everything going on with the loners and so many of the pack still sick with influenza and a number of females now pregnant, I need to know that everything here is being well looked after. I could let Easton go on his own, but—'

'You can't Tobias, I know.' And I do. I've been informed about everything that has happened. He should be with Easton. It's his role as Alpha. Not to mention, Easton does enough for the pack to be respected and supported. 'I'll leave tomorrow.'

Chapter Fifty Eight

Nicolette in Rhiattline

'**B**onita, what are you doing?'

Not turning or acknowledging the males who are standing at the door, I continue to pack. I can scent their exhaustion though and it makes me feel like an absolute bitch. They've been at the hospital all day and for most of the night,

'I have to go back to Farrowline. The alpha called and I'm needed.'

There's a heartbeat of silence. I feel them watching me.

'When?' Luis questions softly.

'Tomorrow morning.'

Why do I feel so sick? And why am I considering delaying my departure? My alpha has asked me home, I need to go. These two didn't think twice when they decided that they'll be leaving for Claymore. I'm sure they never considered me in that decision. They certainly didn't ask for my opinion.

'You can't be serious!' Diego rages. 'My sister is in the hospital after enduring hours of surgery. I just had to look down at her broken body and try to put it back together and I come back to my den to this. I don't need this right now.' He moves into the bungalow and grabs himself a glass and fills it high with water.

My den. The comment has me see red. 'I'm sure the pink bungalow was given to me to stay in while I'm here. It isn't *your* den.'

'Anywhere you are, is my den,' he snaps and I swear I growl. The implication is multi-layered.

'Can we speak about this in a few days, after things have calmed down?' Luis tries to intervene but I'm furious.

'Diego, I'm sorry about Gloria, I've been worried sick all day. I've rung Luis multiple times and have been in contact with my aunt for all the details. So don't make it sound like I'm leaving you without a care.' I'm shaking, I'm so mad. 'My alpha has called me back to pack, I have to go. It's not any different to the announcement you made last night. You're planning to move to Claymore. Why should you be angry at me for leaving when you were going to leave? My holiday is over next week, I was always going to go.'

'You were?' Luis questions softly and I spin around to set my attention on him. Why does he have to sound so dejected?

'Luis—'

'Were you going to leave?' Diego interrupts and I have no idea how I became the bad one here.

'Were you?' I demand, throwing it back in their faces.

'We were discussing it, yes.'

'Exactly,' I bark back.

'What is that supposed to mean?' Diego fires right back.

Waving off the question, I continue to throw things into my bag. The nerve of these males.

'Why don't we calm down, I'll make some coffee and we can have a conversation.' Luis begins to walk to the kitchenette.

'She's already packing, I feel like our mate has already made up her mind!'

Standing tall, I turn around, abandoning my suitcase. My body tenses instantly. My heart barely beats as I register what Diego has just said. 'What did you say?'

'Diego—' Luis sighs heavily.

'You heard me, Nicolette! Don't act like this is some kind of surprise to you. We have spoken our vows to each other. All of us together. You took us as we are, gave yourself to us and bound yourself to this pack the moment you accepted us into your body and your bed. You accepted us and our mating. What do you think we've been doing?'

I open and close my mouth a few times and then realise that every word he speaks rings with truth. A truth that my wolf isn't fighting against. It can't be possible though.

'I didn't say the words. You have to voice a bond like that. I've seen mating happen countless times in Farrowline.'

'I don't think anything about our union is going to follow the same laws as the bonds you see in your pack. You feel the connection between us. You felt the shift that first night we consummated this. We all did.' Luis doesn't raise his voice, but I can hear enough in his tone to know he isn't happy.

'I can't be mated to you both!'

'It's a bit late for that.' Diego growls. I growl. Luis sighs.

Chapter Fifty Nine

Nicolette in Rhiattline

'You were moving to Claymore! You thought I was your mate and you were just going to what, make decisions without even thinking of me!'

'Without thinking of you?' Luis questions. 'All we do is think of you, Nicolette.' Now he is angry. And I'm angry and Diego is pacing again, so he is obviously angry.

'We cannot leave our sister, Nicolette. We can't go to Farrowline with you.'

'I didn't expect you to,' I retort. Luis and Diego share a look that has me burn. 'I know that your sister needs you. Mine needs me. My mother and my pack, they all need me. That is why I'm packing.'

'Gloria has just had major surgery. I need to be close to her. Your pack can surely wait a few days or a week while we set things up, no? Do you not feel the same kind of loyalty to us as we feel for you?'

That has me bare my teeth. 'How dare you question my loyalty.'

The pair are staring at me with anger written all over their faces. A part of me warns that I should stop before I say something I'll regret is shouting in my head but my mouth just keeps going. 'All I do is be loyal to my pack and my family. I never voiced anything, and you question my loyalty? How dare you!'

'How dare we? You're leaving. Packing in the middle of the night with the intent of leaving us. Were you going to say goodbye?'

'Of course I was!'

'If you leave, you leave your mates and your new pack behind, Nicolette.' The words that come from Diego's mouth are like a threat and I don't like threats.

'My pack is Farrowline,' I say without thought. 'I gave everything to them and I'll continue to give everything to them. I could never leave with you both to Claymore or stay here in Rhiattline forever. I have responsibilities and work.'

'Then you have made your decision. You've picked others over your mates.' Diego nods as if the fight has gone out of him.

'You never asked me to stay or follow you to Claymore, Diego.'

He walks out of the bungalow without a backwards glance. I let him go even if the wolf under my skin whimpers for him.

'This is unfair, Luis.'

The dominant male stands at the kitchenette, leaning against the counter staring at me. My normally sweet and calm Luis is seething and I hate it. 'Why are you doing this? What have we done to upset you so much?'

'You haven't done anything. Why don't you both understand? You speak of loyalty but you condemn me for having to go back to my pack to take care of my family and my responsibilities. It makes no sense.'

'But we are your pack now, Nicolette. Diego and I. We are mated. It is us.'

Wow. My entire body freezes. Elation floods my system and yet, no... I can't do that to Farrowline. To...Mama. If she found out that I had mates, that I was secure and thriving, then she'll leave us to follow my father. It has taken so much to get her to the place she is now. Keeping her here is worth giving up everything I ever wanted, including these two.

'My pack is Farrowline. I am a Farrow.'

'Diego is right,' he says as he pushes himself off the counter and strides through the bungalow. 'You hold no loyalty to us. Our mate would never act that way. I guess we were mistaken.'

'I guess you were,' I snap back and hate myself for it.

I pack quickly, fighting the overwhelming grief that has settled in my bones and ring the other Farrowline females who are staying in Rhiattline to tell them that we are leaving the moment the sun rises.

Hating the pounding need to go and find Luis and Diego and also still seething in rage, I slam the door to the pink bungalow and make my way to Aunt El's den.

When she opens the door, she doesn't say anything as she lets me in and sets up the couch for me to sleep on.

The only thing she asks when I silently get dressed for bed and pull the covers over myself is, 'are you sure you know what you're doing, sweetheart?'

She doesn't understand. No one understands. They weren't there in that den when my father died. They don't know the promises I have to keep.

'Yes, I know all too well the consequences of my actions,' is my simple reply.

Chapter Sixty

Present Day

Luis and Diego speak soft words of love as they help me from my clothes and guide me safely into the deliciously hot water in the tube.

I lay my head down on the pillow-towel that Diego has made and stare up at the pair watching me, making sure that I'm all right.

After the adrenaline of the attack and the creek and how they're treating me now, I blurt out, 'you said I was disloyal. You accused me of betraying you both when all I did was listen to my alpha and come home.'

No one speaks. No one moves.

I don't mean to become emotional but everything that has happened and everything that I have to do all comes crashing down on me. I'm so unbelievably tired.

Tears slip down my cheek. They watch them fall in what can only be described as pure pain.

'I did,' Diego confesses after a time and he falls beside the bath. He grips my hand and holds it to his lips. 'And the moment those words came out of my mouth, amor, I have hated myself for saying them. I loathe myself for ever speaking to you in such a way. I can give you reasons of exhaustion and having worked on my sister for hours in that surgery just before I came to you, but it doesn't excuse what I did. What I said. I know I've done the wrong thing. I'm so sorry, mi amor.'

'We both are,' Luis adds, kneeling on the other side of the bath. 'I'd give anything to go back to that night and change what was said. I'm so sorry, bonita.'

Their words have the tears streaming down my face. 'Me too,' I confess. 'I'm sorry. Everything that happened and everything that I said was out of fear of my feelings for you both. Mama and...my head was all over the place.'

'You've experienced great sadness and trauma in your life, Nicolette. We will never ask you to do anything that makes you unhappy. We have you, amor. We see your heart and your soul. The barriers you've created are understandable and we know now.' Diego picks up the sponge and begins to lather my favourite soap on it before he runs it over my shoulders and along my arms. It feels so good.

'Yes, and in that understanding I see you better, Nicolette Farrow. I see the colours of your soul better. You hold everything together and by doing so, you've extinguished your light. Now, we are here to help you burn bright again, bonita. And with us, that is what you can do.' Luis's words hit hard and I gasp and then moan when his fingers, covered in shampoo, begin to massage through my hair. 'We love you.'

'Adore you.'

'Promise to cherish you.'

'And protect you.'

'Promise to keep you from getting lost in work or from building these walls again.'

'And let you be, whatever you want to be.'

'All we ask, is that you do the same for us in return.'

Everything I want to say slips away. I become engrossed in their presence. No more memories haunting me. My grief has been shared and doesn't feel as heavy anymore.

Later, we are all heavy breathing and passion.

Pressed between the two hard, addictive males, I rest the back of my head on Diego's chest and scream their names. The assault on my senses is too much. I feel too much. Luis's hands on my thighs keep me locked around his waist as his thick length draws out my pleasure. Diego is at my back, building the pressure boiling in my veins.

They work in perfect harmony, drawing every moan from my lips, every cry of ecstasy and every mumble of devotion to them.

Chapter Sixty One

Present Day

'I AGREE THAT THERE has been a definite shift in the attacks lately,' Tobias says once Gilly and Delfina conclude their recap of what we suspected last night. No one, especially the males, seem particularly happy that we all faced off with Cade and the loners, but they'll get over it. Not one of them doubts that we had it all covered and handled, which is the main thing.

The Circle dive into a deep discussion of what is happening with the loners and we all agree that things are changing.

'They were watching Cade, Alpha. They smelt...off,' Gilly says thoughtfully and she has our full attention. She tries to elaborate. 'They were related and have bonds like pack, which no loner I've ever met has had.'

'You'll have to explain what that means to everyone, my love,' Oliver informs his mate and Gilly has to take a moment to think.

'We all have bonds of scent and connections and colours that attach us to our environment and to others. For example, I look at Nicolette and I see two thick, dark strands of colours leading from her chest to the distance, where I am sure Luis and Diego are right now.' My jaw hits the floor and it's not the only one. 'There is a green, subtle link between her and Tobias that symbolises their connection. There are countless colours around you, Alpha that links you to everything and everyone, it's actually very beautiful. Each signature scent and marker gives off information.' Gilly looks to the male beside her, seeking reassurance that she has explained herself properly. Oliver nods with that loved-up look on his face.

'You are truly amazing Gilly. You know that, don't you?' Tobias states what we are all thinking and I watch her turn beetroot red in embarrassment.

'Well, what I meant before about how those males are different is that they have colours leading out of them, where loners don't. They seem to cut their ties when they decided to live the way that they do. The two males were very dominant and there was something about them. Their emotions were full of darkness and rage. A hate like I have never smelt before.'

Gilly shivers and we all react by sitting a little straighter, our wolves collectively rising to the surface. Her words make the hair on my body stand on end and I can't help but look around to make sure there are no threats in the area.

'We can only stay vigilant and keep our guard up,' Tobias informs us. 'We have too much going on and I'm worried that we'll have to postpone the mating ceremony again.'

'Not that Ridley would mind,' Jax jokes and it makes us all chuckle because it's true. She hasn't been quiet with how much of a fuss it's all been and how she really doesn't mind if her ceremony just happens at a pack barbecue. That's why we love her.

'Very true,' Tobias states, sounding a bit over the whole thing himself. 'We can't invite all these pack alpha's and humans into our territory when we can't keep them safe.' He rubs at his face as if trying to wipe away the exhaustion. 'There is a part of me that knows that something is coming. That our final clash with the loners is near. I want to just hurry up and get this over with so that we can be free of this torment.'

'I think we would all agree that we feel the same,' Liam replies.

'I guess the only question is, are we truly ready for what is coming?' Jax ponders the question as if he spoke aloud without meaning to.

The quiet that falls is heavy.

Everyone leaves after a time and I'm left sitting across from Tobias who is watching me closely. 'Last night was rough. How are you feeling?'

I scoff at the word he's used. It was more than 'rough'. Last night broke me and then I gave my soul and my heart to Diego and Luis to put it back together. It was…life changing.

'It was a big night.'

'And I noticed that you and your mates were a little calmer this morning.'

'Is there something you want to say, brother?' I snap, ready to be done with this conversation. I really don't want to discuss my sex life with my brother.

'I guess I'm asking if you're going to leave with them?'

It takes me a moment to process. 'What do you mean?'

'Diego made it very clear that he and Luis had to leave in a few days. That his position in Claymore could not be pushed back any longer.'

Tobias's familiar, family eyes bore into mine as I open and close my mouth, trying to find a response.

I don't know what to say. They never mentioned leaving.

Tobias's energy changes and then he is leaning forward, making sure that I'm looking at him. 'Nicolette, if you want to go, then go. Follow your mates. Be happy.'

'Am I not happy?' I fire back, feeling myself getting more and more agitated.

'You tell me.'

'What about Farrow Group? I can't just—'

'But you can,' Tobias interrupts like he knows exactly what I was going to say. He reaches over and places a hand on my knee. 'You have done so much for this pack, Nicolette. I don't think everyone realises just how much you took on when Dad died. You held our family together and you built Farrow Group to what it is today. I've got it covered now if you want to go. You will always be a Farrow and you will always have a position in the company and in the pack, but Nic, go.'

Go.

It is a dismissal and an offer for me to spread my wings.

Go.

But is it that easy?

Chapter Sixty Two

Present Day

Go.

That little word has been playing around in my head. Over and over. It's been two days since the attack and two days since I welcomed Luis and Diego into my heart again.

The memory of what we did last night has me shiver with need and for the hundredth time today I'm distracted from my work. I end up looking out at the cityscape wondering what my life would look like if I did leave. We haven't spoken about Claymore. I think we are all worried to bring it up and popping the bubble we are in right now.

It's given me some time to think about what I want and I found myself unsure.

I think if they were to leave to Claymore...I would follow them. I want to see the world and live my life. I want something new. I want them.

Go.

I'd still be able to work. Most of it can be done remotely. I'd have to change a few things and come back for charity events and client meetings...I'm so conflicted by it all. It's confusing. I thought I'd be mad at myself for contemplating giving up my career for two males, but I don't.

Claymore sounds really appealing. Enticing, actually. I could paint again. I could do some units at the university. I've made enough money to retire and live three lifetimes. And if I'm being really honest, I don't like my job. I didn't do this for the thrills, I did it to support my pack. To pay for my 'crimes'.

August enters the office and goes straight to leaving some papers and messages on my desk.

'The two charity events coming up August, do you think we could send our regrets and apologies?' I ask my assistant who looks up sharply and seems to have some kind of episode.

'Are you leaving us? Is the rumour true?' he outright asks, stunned.

'What rumours?' Fucking hell, shifters are such gossips. August practically dives into the seat across from me, clearly done with working. His focus is locked on me and I see the twinkle in his eye like he's getting the information straight from the source and will probably take it right back to everyone in Farrow Group.

'Oh come on Nicolette, you've hardly been to the office in days. For the last week or so, you've barely answered any calls and you have emails backed up to the hundreds. I had to go in today and manage it all for you. Which you haven't said thank you for yet.' The little jab doesn't do what he expects because he chuckles at my lack of response.

'You get paid better than any assistant in the city,' I remind him.

'I do. But if you leave, what will happen to me?' The shift in his energy has me focus on the male who has managed my life better than I could have.

'I'm not going anywhere, and if I did, I'd still work remotely and will need you, August. You would just see my face more on video.' That seems to pep him up a little. 'But nothing has been decided so it's business as usual.'

I'm not convinced by my own words. August definitely isn't because he nods solemnly and begins to leave the office.

I watch him leaving, knowing that deep down, I may have already made my decision. Going back to what I was trying to do on my computer, I look up when August says, 'you should go, Nicolette. You deserve happiness.'

That takes me off guard. 'August,' I say just before he closes the door. 'You're not just my assistant.' I don't know what else to say.

August smiles. 'I know. You're my friend, Nicolette Farrow and I will always be your friend. You have given me so much and I watch you fund projects and give to charity and help people without batting an eyelid. I hope you find your happiness, even if it means I don't get to come and harass you in your office every day.'

I stare at the back of the door for a few minutes when he closes it behind himself.

It is a few hours later that I finally get what I wanted to do completed after being distracted by my own thoughts all day and tell whoever has just knocked on my door to enter.

Standing near the glass, looking down on the city of Sylo, I spin when I scent the female entering my office.

Mouth hanging open, I can hardly process what I'm seeing.

Mama sits gracefully in the chair on the other side of my desk. She is wearing one of her nicer black, long sleeve dresses and sensible shoes.

'Mum, what are you doing here? You hardly leave Pack.'

'I'm an old female, I'm not den-bound. I leave the Pack when I want to. Ridley came into the office and I tagged along. We need to talk.' My phone buzzes and Mama's entire demeanour changes. 'Don't answer that,' she says before I reach for it. I respect her demand.

'I am here to tell you that I have spoken to your brother and I want to tell you that I agree with what he said. And that I want you to go.'

'Mum—'

'No, Nicolette, I won't sit back and watch you do this. I love you with every fibre of my being and I want to say that I am so sorry, honey.'

I stand in shock, staring at a female who owns my heart completely and who has caused more of the splinters and cracks in it than anyone else. Not that I would ever say that or admit it to her. It was never Mum's fault, but caring for her, making her a priority, it ruined me. It changed me. I made the decisions and I would do it again, but I was so young. 'Mum—'

'No,' Mama cuts me off again. She is solemn and sad. 'Please come and sit down.'

I do what I'm told and sit in my chair and fight the growing emotions playing in my body right now.

'Nic, you've done so much for this pack. So much for me and your sister. Sweetheart, we're okay now. You don't have to stay here if you don't want to. You have two mates who cherish you and you have so much more to give than this.'

She waves her hand around my office, not hiding her disapproval. Mum has never liked what I do.

'I've never kept it a secret that I dislike this job for you. This corporate Nicolette is not who you are. You are my free spirited, creative, artsy pup who drew a forest on the back wall in the loungeroom when you were five. And you did such a good job that your father and I couldn't reprimand you for it.'

Chuckling despite myself, I shake my head. I remember that wall and then sober up when I remember what happened to it. I painted over the forest a few weeks after Dad died.

Mum is watching me closely as if she understands what I'm thinking.

'It was never your fault, sweetheart. What happened to your dad was an act of violence by males who were seeking territory. It is the side of our shifter life that we can not escape. We are animal and human. There are negatives to this world, and you saw that. Your mates know this well and I love that they do, so that they can take care of you properly. They know the pain and they can take some of that from you.'

Mama rises and I don't say a thing. I don't know what to say or how to respond.

'Go, my sweet daughter. Go and live your life. Farrowline will be here for you, whenever you want to visit or come home.'

I don't find the courage to speak until she is almost at the door. 'Will you be here, Mum? If I go?'

Mama turns and I'm met with an expression that breaks my heart. 'Honey, even if I wasn't standing in this room with you now, I will always be here for you, like your father is here, watching and guiding you.'

Chapter Sixty Three

Present Day

I open the door a little dramatically and have the attention of the two males instantly. Luis and Diego are at the kitchen counter, sitting on the bar stools drinking coffee and discussing something, probably how they're leaving soon, without considering me.

'Tell me the plan. I want you to tell me what our lives will be!' I have no idea why I'm angry. Maybe I'm not. Maybe for the first time in a very long time, I'm feeling too much. The walls around my heart aren't solid anymore. They have crumbled and have fallen, useless and no longer keeping me from the crushing weight of what I feel.

'What plan, bonita?'

'The plan to leave for Claymore, for Diego's job. Were you going to include me in the conversation?' I'm being a bitch and I don't care.

They share a look and I find I hate when they do that.

'Nicolette, why don't you come and sit. I'll make you a coffee and we can talk.'

'I don't want to talk.' *What is wrong with me?*

'What do you want to do?' Luis smiles and it's full of mischief.

'Not that,' I snap and even I know that I'm lying. 'I want you to just tell me when you plan to leave and if you were planning on telling more or taking me with you.'

'We would never do anything before discussing it with you.'

'Why would you think we wouldn't include you in that?' Diego questions calmly.

'Because…because, you never asked me to come with you.' Jeez, I sound so pathetic. Who is this Nicolette?

'Mi amor.' Diego sighs and hops off the stool. 'Would you come with us to Claymore?' He is standing right in front of me, his lavender eyes locked on mine. He doesn't touch me. Doesn't do anything but stare.

I respond in my head, in multiple ways. My instinct is to say no but then I don't want to lose this. I don't want to keep going around in circles. I want more. I want to follow my dreams and experience the passion these two offer me.

So, I nod. 'Yes. I want to go with you.'

Diego kisses me so passionately after those words leave my mouth that my knees go all weak and he has to keep me upright by snaking an arm around my waist.

When he pulls away, I am breathless and a little lightheaded.

Once again, I am trapped in those lavender depths, unable to look away. 'Nicolette, we will never leave you again. Where you go, we go and if we all decided to have an adventure in Claymore than we will. If you want to stay here, we will.'

'Okay,' is my simple answer.

He nods and then Luis is pulling me from the taller male so that I crash into his chest, he wraps his scent around me by wrapping his arms across my back. 'If we do go, I have some news.' His energy makes me smile, it is full of excitement and I want to know everything he has to say.

'What news?'

'I have commissioned some work down there and I'll be renting a studio to create some art. So, while Diego will be doing whatever he does, I will be working on some great opportunities. I want you to help me with it. Be part of it. Create with me.' Luis searches my face and I catch my bottom lip between my teeth.

Create with him. Oh, how my life has changed. 'I would love that, Luis.' And I would. The idea of that makes me almost eager to leave.

For the first time, I don't feel bad saying that. I wouldn't turn my back on my responsibilities. Farrow Group can be managed by Tobias and Ridley has become such a powerhouse in the company and she loves it, she'd be thrilled with more.

The future looks scary and new and for the first time it doesn't seem so dark and lonely.

That night I ask August to help me research the logistics of territories to rent and how my life would look if I was to move to Claymore.

Chapter Sixty Four

PRESENT DAY

THE MOOD AROUND THE table is full of energy and laughter. The Circle dinner at Mama's den is in full swing and everyone is having a great time. Luis and Diego are at the other end of the table, laughing and joking with Jax and Mama.

I haven't seen them much today, a passing caress, a kiss while going our separate ways. It's not that I've been ignoring them, it's more that I've been focused on the future, which is very new for me. I'm so used to living in the past and the present. I don't take time, beyond my work schedule, to think about what I want in life. Until now.

After my conversation with Tobias, I can feel the shift in the air. The realisation forming in my mind that I'm leaving. I still have reservations and my stomach flip-flops every time I think of what I'm going to do.

'Mama, are you feeling okay?'

I look up sharply at the tone of Diego's voice. Something is wrong and my suspicion is cemented when I watch as Diego runs his hand up and down Mama's arm while she stares at her plate, not responding.

'Diego?' My heart begins to beat rapidly in my chest.

I'm not sure if it's me or if everyone goes silent, realising the same thing I have, that Mama is still staring at her plate, unmoving.

Diego is speaking to her in that voice that all healers have and I know something is very wrong.

'Mum!' Sara states, her anxiety flows around the table, making the entire den spring into action.

Diego and Tobias are on their feet. Tobias picks Mama up on Diego's instruction and they lie her down on the floor. Dom grabs pillows from the couch while Oliver helps.

Mum's eyes are closed now and the colour has drained from her face. Sara's whimper has me half jump the table to grab her and keep her close to my side. I can't do anything as adrenaline pumps through my veins. There is no enemy for me to fight. No way to release the pressure building in my chest.

'Nic,' Sara pleads and all I can do it hold her tighter.

'Sara, she is okay,' I reassure my sister, making a point of throwing Liam a look. Nodding, Liam takes her and tucks her under his arm. 'What's wrong, Mum?'

'She is all right, aren't you Mama?' Diego replies, I don't know what he says to Luis but the male takes off down the hallway to our room. Mum doesn't answer. I don't think she is conscious.

'Mum!' Shit, Sara sounds like she is about to lose it.

'Liam!' Tobias states just a single word that has Liam coaxing his mate away from the table.

'Adalee,' I say as evenly as I can, the poor woman just stares up at me, her lip between her teeth as she bites it in anxiety. I have no idea where Easton has gone. It is my job to manage this situation and Adalee doesn't need to be here either, especially if there is a problem. She has been through enough. However, before I can get to work making sure that the room is clear and everyone is taken care of, Ridley is up and grabbing for Adalee and Sara. 'Adalee why don't you grab the pups and let's give Diego and Mama some space. Sara, let's go sit outside. I think Nico needs to feed soon and the little ones can play on the equipment.'

Adalee calms instantly and jumps straight into the task of grabbing Gianna and Noah. Liam hands Sara over to our Luna who helps with the pup in her arms as she leads her further outside, where they can still see but be away from the energy.

I don't know how to feel and end up just hovering a few steps away from where Diego is taking Mama's vitals and calmly asking Tobias to assist.

I feel like I'm about to explode. I'm trying not to follow Sara and lose my mind.

'Amor, call an ambulance for me please,' Diego says and I push down the tornado of emotions now boiling in my gut. Diego's lavender eyes rise to my face and I know he sees them all. I can't hide from him. Not since the first day I met him. He has a way of looking at me like he can see every crack and hidden dream. His face softens. 'I am here, Nicolette, she will be okay.'

Nodding, I grip my phone trying to remember how to use it.

'I'll call the ambulance,' Dom states, his hand coming down onto my shoulder to grip it before he disappears outside. There are numerous wolves outside now and I step aside when Kieran and Emma burst through the room.

Everyone starts working on Mama. Luis pulls things from Diego's bag and before my eyes the male turns into the gifted healer that he is.

Frozen in place, I don't know what I'm seeing or what I'm supposed to do. Tobias is helping as much as he can but we aren't healers. So he ends up just standing beside me. His big hand takes mine and I grip it back while praying to the heavens that she is okay.

Chapter Sixty Five

Present Day

I FEEL LIKE I'VE stepped into a nightmare that I can't wake up from. Leg bouncing, I sit, despite the way my body shakes. I watch with everyone else as doctors and nurses come in and out of the swinging doors across the space.

Every time we hear a noise, the mass of shifters in the waiting room almost jump out of their skin to see if it is Diego or Kieran. The healers went with Mama as she was wheeled in, bypassing emergency. She was still unconscious the last time I got a look at her.

Sara is across the room with Liam, Ridley and Adalee. They're keeping her and the pups happy as we wait. I should probably be over there and I would normally be the one to make sure they are all looked after but watching Ridley move around the waiting room, helping Delfina and Easton hand out coffees and snacks or hugging and reassuring everyone has my arse glued to the seat. Luis takes a few snacks and a bottle of water off Gilly when she brings them over to where I sit in the corner. She runs her hand along my shoulder as she quietly walks away to help with Noah.

Tobias is standing just outside the door the doctors keep disappearing behind with Dom. The Alpha is calm and in effect, makes the rest of the room calm. Except, I don't think I'm able to draw on his energy like I should with an alpha. It has my already muddled brain pound harder thinking of that. The only thing keeping me from losing my mind is the male beside me. His solid frame blocks me from half the room and his energy and scent wraps around me

'What would you like to eat, bonita?' Luis shows me the selection of vending machine chip packets and some kind of muesli bar.

'I'm not hungry,' I mumble and go back to watching the door. I was so afraid that this was going to happen. What if after our conversation in the office Mama realised that I was fine now and that she didn't have to stick around. Sara is fine. Clearly, she has some great supporters around her.

Tobias has Ridley, Noah and the pack. I have met my mates. What if that is enough for her to follow my father? I promised that I'd never do this. That I would make sure that she always has a reason to stay.

'Amor, she will be okay. Diego is with her.' He says it like Diego being with Mum will make everything better, and I guess it's true.

'This is all my fault,' I whisper to him.

Luis makes a deep noise of reprimand in his throat. 'It isn't, amor.'

I can't take it anymore. The waiting around for news. The realisation that again I have done something wrong. I rise quickly and hurry from the waiting room with my heart threatening to grumble once more.

I end up outside the tall building, out in the garden, leaning against the brick wall for support.

Tobias appears through the same door I just bashed through and he steps up beside me, mimicking the way I lean on the bricks.

We stand in the quiet darkness.

'It was my job to keep her here with us. To keep her from thinking that we didn't need her anymore,' I say eventually.

Tobias sighs heavily like the weight of my words is crushing. 'For so long, I have watched you lose yourself in work and focus all of your attention on Mama and Sara and I never understood how deeply your guilt went. Not until recently. I'm sorry I didn't support you like I should've. I failed you as your alpha and your brother.'

'You've never failed me, Tobias. I was the one who ran from that clearing and left dad to die on his own.'

The way Tobias's emotions change so suddenly has every hair on my body stand on end. 'Nicolette, what happened to Dad was nothing you could have changed or helped with. They had guns, Nic. They went against every law of our people by not only breaking the laws of a Meet, but by bringing weapons onto our lands. They killed him and if you were there, they would've killed you too.'

A whimper gets lodged in my throat. 'He told me to run and I listened.' I'm crying heavily now and Tobias pulls me into his warm embrace.

'He was your alpha. I would've done the same thing and would've expected obedience. He was your alpha, Nic,' he repeats. 'There was nothing that you could've done to disobey his command. He protected you and I thank the heavens every day that he did because I could never have built this pack to what it is today without you. But this burden you've been carrying around Mama—' Tobias pulls me from his chest and makes sure that I'm looking at him when he says— 'is not going to continue. You cannot live like this and I won't let you.'

'Tobias! Nic!' Dominic calls from the door and we both look up when he indicates that we need to follow.

We rush back to the waiting room and I lock eyes with Diego the moment I return. 'She is okay, mi amor,' he says and Luis is at my side in an instant, gripping my hand. He keeps me grounded.

She is okay.

I draw from Luis' strength to keep myself upright. Relief floods my system.

The collective sigh in the room is audible.

'We suspect she had a transient ischemic attack.' No one reacts and Diego continues to explain that it was like a small stroke. I hear the word stroke and nearly have a heart attack. 'She'll have no permanent damage but she will need to rest and be monitored.'

'Which we will do comfortably back in pack,' Kieran reassures everyone when he comes through the doors. 'She will stay here for tonight and then we will move her.'

Diego leaves our pack healer with Tobias and the others and heads straight for me.

'She is okay. Are you sure?' I ask him, feeling a little hysterical. It all melts away when he grips my arm and pulls me into his chest.

'Mama is fine,' he says to my hair and I throw my arms around him, the other still sits within Luis firm hold, around his thick frame and squeeze him tightly.

'Thank you.'

'You never have to thank me, mate. It is my duty and my honour.'

Chapter Sixty Six

Present Day

Pushing open the back door of Sara's den, I follow the sounds of pups crying and move through the hallway to the kitchen area. I'm expecting Sara to be a complete mess this morning. I'm going to go up to the hospital later and was going to ask Kieran if taking Sara would be a good thing or not. However, when I get to the end of the hall, I stop at what I see.

Ridley is cradling Gianna against her shoulder, consoling the little pup as she slowly stops crying. Sara is feeding Nico on the lounge and sits, watching her Luna with an appreciative look on her face. Ridley has everything under control and Noah is there in an instant when Gianna calms and the Luna places her back down to play.

Adalee is in the kitchen, tinkering around and it appears that she's getting ready to make enough food to feed the entire pack. Just like Mama would do in this situation. She has already made containers of food and packages for the dens yesterday and will do the same today. I can already hear some of the elder females and males who like to cook heading towards the den, drawn to her leadership in this area of our pack. A job Mama held for so long, a job I've seen her slowly relinquish control over.

Like in the hospital yesterday, I observe the way these females are with my sister and realise that she too is all right. That she isn't sitting here crying alone and needing me to come save her. She appears strong and under control. Her pups have her attention and she is supported.

Liam comes through the back door and his gaze fixes straight on me, a true dominant. The females wouldn't have scented me. Sara doesn't have a dominant bone in her body and the other two are human.

I don't know what he sees on my face but he nods, his expression kind and understanding, as if he's telling me that what I'm thinking and feeling is correct. That Sara is okay and being looked after. That she doesn't need me. That I can leave now.

I nod back, feeling tears threatening. I quietly leave the way I came. Tobias is standing at the back door when I push it open and I can't contain them much longer. The Alpha pulls me into his chest and I cry into it, powerless to their force.

I cry because I'm not needed anymore. I cry because I feel a deep sense of relief, which makes me feel guilty as well. I cry because I can finally leave. I've given so much.

'I was never meant to stay here, Tobias,' I confess into his now very wet shirt.

'I know, you were always meant for adventures, and that's okay.' His arms cage me into his mighty body and it feels like a hug from Dad.

Tobias is a true alpha. He pulls back and running his hand down the side of my face, the Alpha of Farrowline smiles warmly down at me. 'You have given so much to this pack, Nicolette. It's okay to hand over the reins. I have it all under control now. This was never your burden to bear. It was mine. I am forever grateful to you for helping me over the years. I couldn't have done it without your support. But you need to leave and follow your heart.'

There is nothing else to say. Not after last night in the garden. I know in my heart what I need to do.

'I don't want to make a big fuss about leaving,' I say and hope that he understands what I have planned.

'I know. I'll tell everyone that you said goodbye.'

'Mama—'

'Will be fine. She comes home today,' he reassures me. 'Ridley and I will take care of her.'

'Farrow Group—'

Tobias smiles down at me. 'Is my company to handle and you will continue to work remotely. We both know you can't give it up. Not right away anyway.'

He is right but I still glare up at him, half-heartedly. 'The loner problem—'

'Is the problem of the Circle of Farrowline. Something that you're not a part of. We both knew why you never accepted it. Deep down you've known all along that Farrowline was not your place in the world. It is your birthpack. Luis and Diego are your pack.' He plants a kiss on my forehead. 'I love you Nic. You are, and always will be, a Farrow. This pack will always be here for you, no matter how far you travel.'

Chapter Sixty Seven

Present Day

I stumble into the sliding doors at Mama's den and fall straight into the embrace of my Luis. He holds me close, not asking me why I'm weeping. Luis just keeps me close, humming me a tune that reassures me that I'm okay, and I believe it. His scent has me thinking of the beaches at Claymore and of the little hut we found in a very beautiful strip of forest and beach that is a mixture between Farrowline and Rhiattline. When Diego found it last night he sent it to me and I filled in the forms to claim the small strip of territory that we will be managing for the next six months, at least. It's wild and liberating to think that I'm going on this adventure with my mates.

'Is it time to go, bonita?' he whispers into my hair.

'Yeah,' I reply softly. 'I think it is.'

He doesn't say any more, he just holds me tighter.

Diego comes through the same sliding doors and takes one look at me and sighs knowingly. 'I'll start packing our bags and getting everything ready.' He doesn't need me to tell him what is wrong, he knows. 'We can always stay a little longer?' he asks over his shoulder just before he disappears down the hall to my room.

'No,' I says softly. 'It's time. As long as you promise that my Mum is okay.'

Face softening, my mate reassures me that she is. 'Your pack is strong, amor. They will miss you, grieve for your absence, but they know you don't belong here. We can come back whenever you want, any time.'

'I know,' I reply feeling a little better. Luis lets me lift my head but he keeps his hold on me. 'I want to do this. I'm actually really excited.'

'So are we, bonita. Together we will build a life of exploration, knowing that we belong to each other and that we are connected to packs around the world.'

Smiling wide enough that my cheeks hurt. 'Actually, there is one thing I want to do before I go. Can you help me with something?'

'Anything,' he states seriously and then returns my grin when I ask him to get his paints.

I walk into the hospital room to see Mama sitting up and eating. The moment she sees me standing at the door, she asks Maree and a few of the other females to give us a moment. They smile as they leave us and I greet them with the respect they deserve being the elders of my birthpack.

The door closes softly behind us and Mama states almost instantly, 'don't you dare use this as an excuse to not leave and follow your mates!'

Laughing despite where we are and where Mama is lying, I move to sit beside her bed. 'Relax Mum, I'm not. I was told that you will be fine.'

'Of course I will be,' she huffs. 'All these dramatics for a silly fainting spell.'

'Mum,' I reprimand in a voice I learnt from her. 'It was more than a fainting spell. You scared us all.' I fuss with her blanket and get slapped away.

'Nonsense.'

'Okay, Mum,' I concede and she glares at my condescending tone.

We sit in silence for a little bit before she says, 'you're leaving, honey, aren't you?'

The tears start the moment I say 'yes.'

I never expected joy to be on my mother's face when I told her that I'm leaving but joy is what I get. 'I'm so happy for you sweetheart.'

'I'm scared, Mum,' I confess, wiping at my stupid tears. I've never cried so much in my life. However, I feel like every drop releases more of the hard exterior that I had constructed to block my pain and emotions. Every tear washes away the mask that I've built. A mask I hate. It's going to take me a while to remember who I am, deep down. The true Nicolette Farrow.

'I know you are and you have to go. When I left Rhiattline once I mated with your father, I was so frightened about the idea of moving to a pack as famous and large as Farrowline. I second guessed my decision. I fought with your father about how unfair it was that I was expected to leave. I made him stay in Rhiattline for two months to prove to me that he would, even though we both knew that he couldn't as the next alpha in line.' She chuckles, clearly remembering something.

While I would've rolled my eyes in the past at Mama's stories of her and my dad, now I find myself understanding. I catch myself thinking of Luis and Diego all the time. It makes me look at my mum differently. The strength this female has. She stayed behind, living a half-life while my dad moved on to the next life without her. The idea of losing either of my mates has me almost hyperventilate. I don't think I'd have the strength to survive their loss. Yet, Mama has endured all these years and I've selfishly held on to her, not allowing her to move on.

'Mum—' I start, wishing I knew what words to use to apologise.

'Darling,' she starts, cutting me off. 'I'm not going anywhere. There are pups I have to help raise and ones that haven't been born yet that I want to meet. I have responsibilities that I take very seriously. Our Luna still needs me. Do I long for your father? Of course I do. Do I wish he were here? Every day. But he and I understood that pack and family comes first. I'm a Luna. I don't have the luxury of giving up and leaving this life, not yet. I want to see where life takes you, I've already planned with Maree that we will come visit Claymore in the summer.'

I laugh out loud and wipe my face. I hope Diego and Luis are ready for my family to come and use our den like their own.

Who am I kidding, it was probably their idea.

Mama leans over and I move to meet her halfway and close my wet eyes when her hand cups the side of my face. She is warm. Safe. Healthy.

'Leave sweetheart. Go and live your life and I will be here if, and when, you need me. I still have some life left in me. It's now your time to go live your life and be who you were meant to be. My free-spirited daughter. Shine brightly.'

Chapter Sixty Eight

Present Day

WE DECIDE TO LEAVE after I get back from the hospital and while I was hoping to slip away quietly, the moment Diego opens the front door to Mama's den, my heart stills in my chest.

Luis' hand falls to the small of my back as I take a moment to compose myself. Every single member of Farrowline is standing quietly on Mama's front lawn, staring at me.

Some dab their eyes, others nod their heads as I follow Diego down the steps and along the front footpath, past all the rose bushes and the cars in the driveway to my left.

My pounding heart is the only thing that can be heard. Sara and Liam standing with their pups at the end of the path, just beside the car we will be taking to Claymore.

Sara hugs me firmly with Nico between us.

'I would say that you have to call me every day but we both know you will, even if I said it or not.'

I laugh softly, drawing in her scent, one last check to make sure she is okay before I leave. 'I'm okay Nic, you can go. Thank you for being such an amazing big sis. I love you. I'm sorry if I was the reason you stayed here so long.'

'No, honey. Never. I love being your big sister.'

Sara laugh-cries. 'I saw the wall you re-painted. Mum is going to cry when she sees it. She loved that wall. We were all so sad when you painted over it.'

'I'm sorry,' I whisper, hating that I hurt them all. I painted over the forest I made as a pup, in a fit of emotion, just after Dad died.

Sara tsks and it's such a motherly sound. 'You were grieving. What you and Luis created is just beautiful, Nic.'

It really is. Luis and I painted Farrowline on Mama's wall last night. We captured the entire landscape.

Diego watched us the entire time and we all discussed our plans for the future and the pains of our past. It was perfect.

'I love you, honey,' I whisper into her hair and kiss it one last time before giving some love to Gianna and Nico.

Liam hugs me tightly, telling me that I'm free to the leave the pack knowing all will be taken care of.

'We have it covered,' Dom reassures me with a big kiss on the cheek.

'You ring me if something happens, or you need me to come and crack some skulls,' Delfina states, her hazel eyes are serious and I know that she speaks the truth.

I can't help but grin and promise.

Oliver and Gilly are next, both informing me that they will be down in the summer to enjoy the sand and sun with Mama. Adalee hands over a container of food and Easton hands over a bag with more treats and containers. It's more than we can consume. 'Thank you Adalee,' I say and hug her and Easton together.

Jax comes up last. The handsome monster of a male picks me off my feet when he hugs me. 'I can't wait to hear of your adventures. And I'll get that report to you on Monday for the Huston account,' he says sheepishly and I scoff and make everyone laugh. I asked him for that report two weeks ago.

'You have until Monday,' I warn and nod when Diego tells me it's time to go.

I turn to the door and come face-to-face with my brother.

There are no more words to be said between us. He hugs me tighter than anyone else. 'Safe travels. I'll see you on our video conference on Monday morning.'

That has us all laugh again. 'Yes, Tobias.'

'I'm going to miss you,' Ridley states and throws her arms around me.

'I'm going to miss you too, Luna. You have everything under control here now though.'

She pulls back and I get the full force of her chocolate human shaped eyes. For a non-shifter she sure has the energy of an alpha. 'I do, Nic.' She says the words like a promise and I know she does.

Without another word, I let Diego help me into the front seat. Doors are closed. Luggage is packed into the boot and I wave a small goodbye, watching Farrowline and the shifters I call family slip by.

'You okay, bonita?' Luis asks from the backseat. He sits forward as best he can with his guitar on his lap.

Diego's hand slips off the steering wheel and takes the one I have balled on my leg.

Smiling up at them both, I nod. 'Yeah, I am.'

'Are you ready for our first adventure, mate?' Diego asks, my chest fills with emotions.

'Our first of many?' Luis adds and I inhale and exhale for what feels like the first time since my father was taken from me.

'Yes.'

Luis and Diego make a deep sound in the back of their throats that has my thighs clench and my own wolf rise to the surface.

Laughter fills the inside of the vehicle as we all realise that this is going to be a long trip with many, many stops along the way.

Luis strums his guitar and the laughter is replaced with his voice. Diego joins in during the first chorus and by the end, I too have pushed away the reservations and the fear. The mask that I created slips away for good and I join my voice with theirs.

TO BE CONTINUED

BOOK 6 OF
THE PACK OF FARROWLINE
SERIES

COMING SOON

The content of this book is a product of the author's imagination, memory and/or original research and was not generated with the use of AI (artificial intelligence). While some generally acceptable publishing industry tools such as spelling and grammar checkers, formatting tools, design and layout tools etc., will have been used to help improve the reader's experience and develop the manuscript into a book, this work is original content inspired and generated by the author and their creativity. As such, the author would like to thank you for supporting their efforts in this regard.

ABOUT THE AUTHOR

A L Rojo is an author, educator, wife and mother who lives in Sydney, Australia. From a young age, she understood the power of getting lost in a good book. After giving herself permission to explore her creativity, she found that she loved writing novels that focus on strong female characters, love, spice, and the wonderful complexities of life. Her goal is to simply create worlds where anyone can escape into, for however long they may need. She says that along this journey she has left behind a piece of herself in every character she creates.

To get the latest updates, follow A L Rojo and The Pack of Farrowline below.

Website: www.alrojo.com.au
Facebook: A L Rojo
Instagram: alrojo_writer

www.ingramcontent.com/pod-product-compliance
Lightning Source LLC
LaVergne TN
LVHW041621060526
838200LV00040B/1386